Please, God, keep her safe.
Let me get to her in time.

Jackson spied Alyssa's car before he realized he'd reached a dead end. What could she be doing out here? He parked the truck alongside her car and leaped to the ground.

Cupping his hands around his mouth, he hollered her name.

He waited, measuring the silence. No birds tweeted. No cicadas chirped. Odd for here in the bayou. Taking a slow turn, he studied the terrain. Woods, bushes. A trail.

With impressions of fresh footsteps. About Alyssa's size.

Jackson headed down the trail, quickening his pace. If his bearings were dead on, which they normally were, he'd run right into the swamp. Really close to the money drop site.

"Alyssa. Alyssa," he called again.

A woman's scream pierced the air.

Books by Robin Caroll

Love Inspired Suspense

Bayou Justice #74
Bayou Corruption #89

ROBIN CAROLL

Born and raised in Louisiana, Robin Caroll is a Southern belle right down to her "hey, y'all." Her passion has always been to tell stories to entertain others. Robin's mother, bless her heart, is a genealogist who instilled in Robin the deep love of family and pride of heritage—two aspects Robin weaves into each of her books. When she isn't writing, Robin spends time with her husband of eighteen years, her three beautiful daughters and their four character-filled cats at home—in the South, where else? An avid reader herself, Robin loves hearing from and chatting with other readers. Although her favorite genre to read is mystery/ suspense, of course, she'll read just about any good story. Except historicals! To learn more about this author of Deep South mysteries of suspense to inspire your heart, visit Robin's Web site at www.robincaroll.com.

ROBIN CAROLL

BAYOU CORRUPTION

Steeple
Hill®

Published by Steeple Hill Books™

STEEPLE HILL BOOKS

Steeple
Hill®

ISBN-13: 978-0-373-44279-9
ISBN-10:   0-373-44279-3

BAYOU CORRUPTION

www.SteepleHill.com

Printed in U.S.A.

Cast all your anxiety on Him because
He cares for you.
                              —*1 Peter* 5:7

To Emily Carol, Remington Case &
Isabella Co-Ceaux
For all the times you let Mommy work
And celebrated with me…
I love you THIS much,
Mommy

Acknowledgments

Most sincere thanks to my editor, Krista Stroever, who used her brilliance to make this book stand out. To my agent Kelly Mortimer, my biggest fan. Thank you both for believing in me and this series.

Thanks to Colleen Coble—your encouragement and praise, and threat of a pickax, motivate me!

I thank my wonderful CPs—Dineen, Heather, Ron, Camy and Ronie. And Cheryl for love, prayers and support.

Thanks to Tracey, Lisa and Cindy for pointing out inconsistencies.

Thanks to my family: my husband, three girls, Grannie & Papa, Rebecca and Bubba for the support & encouragement.

Big thanks to the members of ACFW, whose support and encouragement of me as president has truly been one of the biggest blessings of my life!

Finally, my most humble thanks to my husband, Case. I love you, always.

All glory to my Lord and Savior, Jesus Christ.

PROLOGUE

"I really need your help, buddy." The voice of Jackson's old frat brother was concerned and wary.

Jackson clenched the phone tightly and stared at his calendar. He had more than a month's vacation time coming. Lagniappe just wasn't a prime vacation spot in his opinion. "But why do you need *me?* Can't one of your deputies help you on the case?"

"That's the problem. I think I've got a mole. Every new bit of information I uncover seems to fall into the wrong hands." Bubba sighed heavily. "Please. I can't trust anybody here. I need an outsider, someone nobody knows."

"What, exactly, can I do?"

"You're a reporter—you have the skills to ferret out the truth. You can dig around unnoticed, and since you'll only be giving *me* the details, there isn't a chance for leaks."

Jackson contemplated his options half-heartedly. From the moment he'd answered the phone and heard his friend's worried voice, he'd known he'd go to Lagniappe, Louisiana, and help out if he could. And it very much looked as if he could.

"I'm not gonna lie to you, Jacks, I really believe there's some sort of smuggling going down on the intercoastal port. I've found two money drops in the bayou, and you know that's common with smugglers. You and I both know how dangerous this situation can be."

Now there was an understatement. Smugglers would lie, cheat, steal and even kill to protect their stakes. But Jackson thrived on adventure and danger. He headed to his bedroom and grabbed a duffel. "I'll be there in two days."

ONE

Even Mother Nature hated Lagniappe, Louisiana.

Ominous fall storm clouds hung low in the sky. A bright spear of lightning flickered across the sky, then the earth trembled—positives and negatives of nature colliding.

The glass doors to the parish hospital rattled. Alyssa LeBlanc darted into the old building, drenched and shivering. Why hadn't she thought to bring her umbrella? The smell of disinfectant and illness assaulted her senses and memories. She almost gagged. Her heels tapping briskly, she made her way to the nurses' station. She imagined death dogging her every step.

"Pardon me, what room is Marie LeBlanc in?"

The nurse glanced over the counter, eyes hardening and the corners of her mouth slicing down. "Visiting hours are long over." Her gaze drifted over Alyssa, disapproval lining her plump face as she took in Alyssa's chic business slacks and silk blouse.

Alyssa straightened her shoulders, despite the burning cramp caused from six hours behind the wheel. "I was called—she's my grandmother." She offered a shaky smile. Maybe Nurse Ratched would have a heart.

Wonder of wonders, her tactic worked. The older

woman let out a heavy sigh and softened her expression. "Room 112, just down the hall to the right. You can only see her for a minute."

"*Merci.*" Alyssa turned on her four-inch heels and strode down the hall. Not even back for an hour and already falling into the old speech patterns. She shook her head. No, she wouldn't let Lagniappe smother her again. Not when she had a hot assignment that could launch her career waiting back home.

Halting at the door of Room 112, she reached in her pocket for her lip balm. She applied a thick coat, paying special attention to the burning scar just on the edge of her lower lip, and slid the tube back into the pocket of her slacks before pushing open the door.

Light spilled into the darkened room from the hall behind her. Only a small beam glowed over the hospital bed. Two machines on either side—their beeps low and hypnotic—illuminated the patient lying flat. Alyssa's legs moved as if the floor were swampland. Her heartbeat pounded in her throat as she studied the frail form lying so still. Why hadn't her sister called sooner? Their grandmother looked as if she were knocking on death's door.

A strange feeling rose within her, enveloping her like lichen on bayou trees. A sense of warning, of caution. She shook off the sensation and picked her way across the room on tiptoe. The metal railing felt cold to her touch, but no chillier than the regret seeping into her spirit. "Oh, Grandmere."

Her grandmother's eyes flicked open.

Had she spoken aloud?

"Alyssa, *ma chère,* is that you?" Grandmere lifted a gnarled hand.

"Oui." She took her grandmother's hand in her own. When had Grandmere's skin turned as thin as parchment? "I came as soon as CoCo called."

"I told her not to. I'm fine. This is just a little episode."

The pale skin beneath the tan from the outdoors told a different story. Alyssa swallowed. "I'm glad she did." Her voice hitched, but maybe Grandmere wouldn't notice.

"Ma chère, I'm well. She shouldn't have bothered you. I know you're busy with your paper." The coloring wasn't the only thing off about Grandmere—those mere three sentences stole her breath. She shifted on the bed, a wheezing noise hissing from her chest. Grandmere reached for the rail with her free hand, the one with an IV.

Alyssa helped lift her grandmother into a sitting position, her head and her heart warring. She needed to pursue her career, and she had. She'd worked her way up from obits and social events to investigative reporter. Her mother had been the star photojournalist for the New Orleans *Times-Picayune.* One day, Alyssa would nab the position they'd denied her there twice. But seeing her grandmother like this…

A cough racked her grandmother's body, bouncing off the drab white walls and filling Alyssa with foreboding.

"I'm okay." Grandmere slumped against the pillows, her face ashen. A thin layer of sweat beaded her upper lip.

Grabbing a tissue from the box on the bedside table, Alyssa swallowed back the guilt. She dabbed her grandmother's face. Grandmere rewarded her with a soft smile, but didn't open her eyes. "I just lose my breath oft times."

"It's okay." She tossed the tissue into the bedside trash can and noticed several other wads. "When does your doctor make rounds in the morning?" She certainly had a couple of issues to discuss with him regarding her grandmother's condition.

"Now you sound like CoCo, *ma chère.* He'll be here around nine-ish."

The door whooshed open, and a nurse stood with her hands on her ample hips. "You have to leave now. My patient needs her rest." She made her way to the bed. Her hands smoothed the covers over Grandmere before plumping the pillows.

Alyssa planted a short kiss on her grandmother's temple. "I'll see you in the morning."

"You be careful now, *chère.* I've been listening to the thunder. The spirits aren't too happy."

Those spirits again. Here Grandmere lay in the hospital following a mild heart attack, supposedly, and concern over unhappy spirits filled her thoughts. If she had such a connection with the spirits, why hadn't they warned her about her ailing health? Some things never changed, but now wasn't the time or place to get into *that* discussion. Alyssa nodded and backed out of the room.

She pressed against the wall, cold seeping into her skin through her soaked blouse. She'd had no idea Grandmere was so bad off when CoCo had called this morning. If she had, she wouldn't have lingered at the paper, begging her editor not to give the new juicy assignment to her rival. Alyssa shook her head and strode toward the parking lot. No matter that she'd dallied. She'd make the most of her time with Grandmere this weekend before getting back to work in Shreveport on Monday.

Darkness lurked over the parking lot, and the rain came down in sheets. Something chilly hung in the air tonight, even though South Louisiana stayed warm through September. Alyssa berated herself for forgetting her umbrella. Rushing to the car, she noted that four streetlamps were out. Figured. Lagniappe couldn't even change their light bulbs. No big surprise. She sank into the driver's seat of her Honda, resting her forehead on the steering wheel. Droplets plopped onto her lap.

What had she let herself in for, coming back? Hadn't she vowed not to return? Cajun country had stolen everything near and dear to her more than a decade ago—her parents, her home in New Orleans, her normal life. She'd been ridiculed because of her grandmother and older sister, making her social life, if it could even be called that, miserable.

Only the rain pounding against the windshield answered her. She cranked the engine, flipped the defroster on high, and jerked the car into gear. Hopefully, CoCo would have a nice pot of coffee simmering at the house.

She steered onto the main road leading out of town. Town in the same breath as Lagniappe? Now that was an oxymoron. Alyssa shoved down her thoughts. She clicked on the radio, found a jazz station and turned up the volume. She only had to stick it out for a weekend. She'd see Grandmere safely back home before heading back to Shreveport. Only three days. She could survive this.

The wipers squeaked against the windshield, seeming to keep time with the music on the radio. Alyssa hunched over the steering wheel. Up ahead lay the turnoff to the LeBlanc homestead. She slowly applied her brakes, but hit a slick spot of mud. The car slid toward a ditch. The cypress trees with Spanish moss hanging low blurred as the car spun. She jerked the wheel. Overcorrected, the car gyrated. She pressed the brakes, hoping the antilocks would kick in, but the car picked up momentum and headed for the gully. With a jar, her car landed nose first in the ditch. The Honda's engine died and the headlights went dim. Not a total loss—the jazz still blared from the speakers.

Now what? She turned off the radio, twisted the key to restart the car and pumped the accelerator. Nothing but a whirring noise sounded over the din of the rain. She pressed the lights off. No sense wasting her battery. Digging around in the console, she located her cell phone and flipped it open. One bar. She punched in her sister's number, but the call wouldn't go through. SERVICE NOT AVAILABLE. Just her luck.

Taillights dotted the darkness not more than fifty yards next to her on the road to the house. Drawing in a breath, she grabbed the door handle and stepped into the driving rain. Ahead, the car's brake lights flicked on. Maybe they'd seen her; maybe they could help. She ran toward the vehicle as fast as she could in her spike heels. The mud sucked at her feet, making popping sounds.

Two figures emerged from the car. Goosebumps pimpled Alyssa's back, and she froze. That odd sense of foreboding she'd experienced at the hospital returned with a vengeance. Something inside screamed *Caution!* She shivered and slowed her pace, trying to see the figures more clearly through the onslaught of rain.

They struggled to maneuver something big and bulky from the backseat. A voice carried on the wind. "Hurry up, we don't want to be seen." A man's voice, deep and edgy, a voice she'd never forget. Alyssa's insides bunched and she held her breath.

"...heavy," a second voice replied, followed by a large grunt.

Alyssa crouched to the side of the road, cold mud covering her shoes. Her heart thumped so loud, surely the men would hear the pounding. They didn't. Whatever they took from the backseat hit the road with a loud thud. The two figures hopped back into the car and sped away. Alyssa tried to make out the license plate, but the rain and the speed of the car blurred the numbers.

When the taillights disappeared from view, Alyssa inched up to the big bag sitting in the middle of the road. Probably trash. Just like the rednecks in this backwoods town. More likely, teens in Daddy's Pontiac. At least that's what she tried to convince herself. She focused on what she recalled. She thought the car had been a Pontiac. Metallic blue, from what she could make out from the brake lights' illumination.

The closer she got, the larger the sack became. The least they could've done was dump the bag on the side of the road so an unsuspecting motorist wouldn't run into the thing.

Alyssa looked up and down the dark road. Not a car in sight to help pull her out of the ditch. No nice, calm driver with a normal voice. Unlike the one that sent shivers tickling her spine.

Soaked to the bone, she'd come this far so she might as well see what they'd dumped. She rushed forward before common sense could make her change her mind, grabbed the end of the black industrial-grade bag and tugged. It didn't budge. Alyssa gripped the edges tighter, but her wet hands slipped. She gave the sack a hard jerk.

It groaned.

She flinched hard, nearly toppling over. Her heart jumped against the back of her throat. Did that bulging bag really moan and move?

Another loud groan.

Oh, mercy sakes alive, they'd dumped a body. A live one!

She scratched at the bag, fighting to puncture the material with her nails. Strong stuff, but she kept on clawing, chipping her manicure, until she ripped the sack open. Her stomach bunched into tight knots as she realized the condition of the body. She freed the person's face from the plastic.

And gasped.

She barely recognized the man. After all, it'd been three years, but the red hair gave away his identity. Sheriff Bubba Theriot lay inside, bleeding and battered. His breathing came in short puffs, shallow and labored. She grabbed his wrist and checked his pulse—thready and faint.

"Hold on, Sheriff. I'll call for help." She ran to her car, her heels sinking into the marshy mud. Alyssa caught herself on the car door, and fell into the seat. Her hands trembled as she grabbed her cell phone.

Please, let me get reception out here in the boondocks.

Still only one bar—not enough to make a call. Alyssa hesitated over the button to the hazard lights. Would the men come back? They had no reason to suspect they'd been observed. Surely they wouldn't be so stupid to return to the scene of the crime. Then again, they *had* left him alive. What if they decided to come back and make sure he'd died? Right or wrong, she had to do something. She flipped on the hazard lights, grabbed the flashlight from the backseat and headed toward the sheriff, holding her cell phone open.

Just another bar. Just one more.

About ten yards from the sheriff, the phone beeped. She held the display closer to her face. Two bars out of five. Not the best, but she should at least get a 911 call out. Sure enough, the dispatcher answered and asked the nature of her emergency.

"It's the sheriff. His body. I mean, he's still alive, but just barely." Sobs tore from her throat. She fought against them, swallowing hard, but the tears wouldn't be denied. She ran a finger over her scar, which felt hot to her touch.

The dispatcher took down the location before assuring Alyssa help would be there soon.

Alyssa shoved the phone into her pocket with shaking hands and rushed to the sheriff's side. Rain washed the blood from his face. Bruises littered his flesh. Gashes and cuts. Crooked and bleeding nose. His swollen eyes opened and locked on her face. Her gut twisted. This was worse than covering the five-car pileup on I-30 last month.

"D-Don't let…th-them get…away…with…it…Jacks." His lids closed and his breathing shallowed out even more.

Jacks? Delirium must have set in. She smoothed the hair off his forehead, careful to avoid the deep cuts. Her hands trembled. Who would do such a thing? She glanced over her shoulder, apprehension settling over her as fast as the rain soaking her blouse. Alyssa swallowed and prayed, even though she wasn't sure what to say to the God she visited once a month.

Please let the ambulance get here in time. Don't let this man die. Not while I'm here, God. Not again. Please.

Squawk! The police scanner squealed to life.

Jackson Devereaux bolted upright on the couch, popping his knuckles as he blinked away the grogginess. He'd forgotten the box was on. Seldom did anything

come over the airwaves. No one could ever call Lagniappe a hoppin' town.

His jaw dropped as he listened to Missy, the dispatcher,
call out a frantic plea. Bubba? Needing an ambulance?
He jumped to his feet and snatched his keys and Black-
Berry from the kitchen table, hovering by the scanner. An
address—he needed the location.

Missy provided the details in a shaky voice, not at
all her normal upbeat self. In her early thirties and
having done the dispatching job for over a decade,
Missy shouldn't be rattled. That she sounded frantic...
well, Bubba must be in serious need. Jackson raced
from the house, leaped into the truck and gunned the
engine.

She'd given sketchy information at best. Bubba, in-
jured badly enough to need an ambulance, out in the
middle of nowhere. Jackson went over the directions
again as he sped into the pelting rain.

Something smelled foul in the bayou, and it wasn't the
gar washing up on the banks.

His friend's troubles were linked to the case they were
working on—Jackson sensed it strongly. He jerked the car
onto a side road, choosing not to slice through the town
square. He used the term loosely—coming from New
Orleans, he'd laughed when Bubba had proudly taken
him around the downtown area. Small towns didn't
exactly have the excitement he'd become accustomed to.
Then again, if what Bubba suspected were true, there'd
be a lot of unrest hitting Lagniappe.

Hazard lights blinked just off the main road. He eased
up on the gas, letting the weight of the truck carry him
forward. A woman staggered to her feet just past a ditched

car. The rain plastered her short hair to her head, making her eyes seem to jump off her face.

After parking the truck on the side of the road, he turned on his own hazards and flipped on his high beams. He approached the minute woman. She took a defensive stance, as if she could fight him off with the flashlight she held if he'd intended her harm. Shorter than him by almost a foot, she couldn't be more than a hundred pounds, soaking wet.

"Wh-who are you?" The pixie lifted a yellow, square DeWALT flashlight and shined the beam into his eyes.

Jackson strode toward her. "I'm a friend of Bubba's. Who're you?"

She cocked her head to the side, as if sizing him up, and stumbled backward a step. "How do you know about him?" Her clipped tone, full of suspicion, drifted to him over the rain. She hadn't answered his question.

No time for proper introductions. "I'm his houseguest. Police scanner. Bubba keeps it turned on all the time." He knelt beside his friend.

Bubba's face looked as if it'd been used as a punching bag. Jackson clenched his jaw. Hard. "Pard, what happened to you?" he mumbled.

His response must've convinced her that he wasn't a mass murderer as she knelt beside him. "He hasn't moved since he tried to talk to me."

Jackson laid two fingers on Bubba's neck. Slow pulse, and not at all steady. His friend's eyes were swollen to the point where he couldn't open them if he'd tried. "What happened? What'd he say?"

The woman's round brown eyes looked too large for her face. Or maybe they only appeared that way as she spoke with such animation. "I was heading ho—uh, to my sister's house and actually slid into the ditch." She nodded toward the car a couple hundred yards away with the yellow lights blinking. "A car pulled out of nowhere. I ran over, thinking I'd ask for help. But I heard men's voices, and something about them told me to stop."

He could sense her tension even as Bubba's skin turned cold and clammy. Why hadn't he thought to grab his windbreaker?

"I saw brake lights. Two figures took something from the backseat and tossed it in the road. One told the other to hurry, and the other complained that the bag was heavy." She lowered her gaze to settle on Bubba's face. "I thought they dumped trash."

His friend, tossed in a bag and thrown onto the road like garbage? He glanced at Bubba's broken form. Beaten and left for dead. What if this woman hadn't found him?

"I tried to move the bag to the side of the road, so no one would round the curve and hit it." Tears mixed with the rain on her cheeks. "I couldn't. Then I heard him moan." A shudder coursed over her.

She'd most likely saved Bubba's life. Jackson laid his other hand over hers and squeezed. "What'd he say?"

Sirens lashed out against the silence. Blue flashing lights strobed against the moonless night.

She jerked her hand free of his grasp and pushed to her feet. "About time they got here. I've been praying they wouldn't be too late."

Jackson didn't have time to comment before the police cruiser, trailed by a parish ambulance, sloshed to a stop. A deputy pulled him and the woman away from Bubba to talk while the paramedics made record time getting his friend into the ambulance. They sped off before Jackson could even ask the paramedics about the extent of Bubba's injuries.

The interior of the police car reeked of stale cigarette smoke. Jackson glanced at the woman crammed into the backseat beside him. Her gaze lit on his face, revealing something so sweet…so pure. He smiled, although the little voice in his mind wondered when had a pretty, helpless woman not turned his head.

The deputy, introduced as Gary Anderson, shifted in the front seat to stare at the two of them. "Now, let's start at the beginning." He nodded to the woman. "You are?"

"Alyssa LeBlanc. I'm a—"

"Wait a minute. Alyssa…are you CoCo's sister?" Gary asked.

Alyssa. Brought to mind a little fairy. Jackson studied her for a minute. Yeah, the name suited her.

She nodded. "I live in Shreveport and drove down this afternoon because my grandmother had a heart attack."

"Yeah, I heard. Sorry 'bout that. How's she doing?"

"Okay."

Jackson cleared his throat. "Could we please get on with this so I can go to the hospital and check on Bubba?"

"Just hold yer horses." The deputy scrawled on a little notebook. "So, Ms. LeBlanc, tell me what happened."

Alyssa repeated what she'd told Jackson.

"Did you recognize the car?" the deputy asked.

"No. It was metallic blue, though. At least, that's how it looked in the light from the brakes. And a Pontiac, I think."

She'd never mentioned the make or color of the car before. Jackson looked hard at her.

"Did you recognize the men?"

"No, but I haven't lived here in a long time, and it's raining pretty hard." She laced her hands in her lap. "I crouched down near the side of the road so they wouldn't see me." She shivered. "They gave me the creeps."

"Would you recognize their voices again if you heard them?"

She shuddered and nodded. "One of them, most definitely."

"Tell me what the sheriff whispered to you."

Jackson hadn't gotten an answer to that, either.

Alyssa pinched her eyes shut. "He said, 'Don't let them get away with it, Jacks.' Then he lost consciousness."

Jackson stiffened his shoulders. His gut instinct was right—the investigation Bubba had called him in to help on was directly linked to this attack. Now he had to figure out who was behind everything.

The deputy kept writing in his notebook. "Any idea what he referred to?"

"Not a clue."

Deputy Anderson nodded before facing Jackson. "Now, sir, you are?"

"Jackson Devereaux. I'm a friend of Bubba's. His houseguest."

"Oh, yeah?"

Jackson let the question die and explained how he'd heard the news on the police scanner and rushed over.

"Why'd you do that?"

"He's my friend."

"Most people don't listen to police scanners." The deputy stared at him a moment, disbelief etched into the tiny wrinkles around his eyes.

"It's Bubba's scanner."

The deputy huffed and turned to Alyssa. "Do you listen to police scanners, ma'am?"

A slow smile crept across her face. "Actually, I do." She held up a finger. "But I'm a newspaper reporter and that's what we do."

A reporter. His competition.

"Uh-huh." The deputy focused back on Jackson. "Does what the sheriff said to Ms. LeBlanc mean anything to you?"

Jackson fidgeted in the seat. No sense not being upfront—it'd all come out soon enough. "Yeah. Bubba calls me Jacks."

TWO

Yet another reason to detest this horrid bayou—a two-hundred-dollar pair of heels, ruined. She'd scrimped and saved for three months to buy them. As if she didn't already have enough cause for irritation after tonight.

Alyssa tossed the shoes onto the floorboard of the passenger side of the car. Maybe the dry cleaners could work some miracle on them when she got back to Shreveport. No, when she got back *home*.

Shivers raced up and down her spine while she stared in her rearview window. That scene had rattled her more than she cared to admit. Some seasoned reporter she was turning out to be. Mr. Devereaux hooked his truck's winch to the back of her car, then slapped her trunk. She slipped the gear into Neutral and gripped the steering wheel, ready to guide the car from the ditch. At least she didn't have to wait for a tow truck.

Deputy Anderson kept a careful eye on Mr. Devereaux's actions, standing alongside him. The police might question Mr. Devereaux's involvement in the attack because the sheriff had said his name, but her journalist's instinct screamed a big *no*. If he'd attacked the sheriff, why'd he come to help? It didn't make sense. Unless he came back to finish the job. No, that couldn't be right. Different vehicle, different voice.

Mr. Devereaux was handsome with his curly, dirty-blond hair and his dark, haunting eyes. The eyes that seemed to see into her soul. Something about the shape of them… She knew she'd seen them before but couldn't place where. Even his name sounded vaguely familiar. As soon as she got a chance, she'd Google him. She might not recall where she knew him from, but she had a strong feeling she hadn't liked him. No matter how good-looking.

The car jerked and slowly rolled backward. Alyssa turned the wheel until her Honda sat in the middle of the road. When the car stopped moving, she set her stocking-clad foot on the brake, dried mud granules digging into the pad. In her side mirror, she watched Mr. Devereaux unhook her car. He wound the cable back onto the winch of the truck he drove, then appeared at her window. She let the glass down a couple of inches.

"Crank 'er up." Mr. Devereaux hadn't even gotten winded coiling the heavy metal cable. Macho man.

She turned the key. The engine purred. "Thank you so much."

"Happy to help."

"Well, I'd better get to my sister's. I bet she's worried about me."

"Do you want me to follow you, just to make sure you arrive okay?"

"No." Realizing she'd snapped the word, she forced a smile. Where were her manners? "No, thank you. It's not that much farther." She glanced in her side mirror. "Besides, I think the deputy's waiting on you."

"Drive safely, *chère.*"

Alyssa closed the window before putting the car in gear. Careful to drive slowly, she kept both hands firmly on the wheel. She glanced in her rearview mirror. Mr. Devereaux's and the deputy's brake lights glowed faintly in the distance.

The rain's intensity diminished, but an ominous sensation seemed to hover over her. As if someone were watching her. Alyssa shuddered. She stiffened her spine and gripped the steering wheel tighter. Probably just her imagination, her unease at being back in the bayou.

She stared at the plantation home through the rain-streaked window. The house that had stood since before the War Between the States, her father's childhood home, the place she'd been banished to when her life flipped upside down and where she suffered her worst humiliations as a teenager. Kudzu wove around the outside of the house, and the drooping branches of the live oaks formed a canopy entrance from the driveway. Alyssa swallowed and reached for the handle of the car door. She couldn't put this off any longer. She grabbed her overnight case and headed to the veranda.

Mud oozed up through the nylon between her toes. Disgusting. She grimaced but kept going. A gust of wind swept over the bayou, lurking to the right of the house behind Grandmere's shed. The bright blue paint from the small lean-to drew attention away from the white of the big house. Steps creaked under her stocking feet as she made her way to the porch. She noticed the random new boards, not yet treated to match the others. At least CoCo attempted to keep up with maintenance.

She paused at the front door. Should she knock? Technically, she had as much right to the house as her sisters.

Yet, she'd turned away—fled, more accurately—from the place almost nine years ago. She'd only returned three times in the past five years, for Christmases, and during the last visit, when she'd run into one of the do-gooders who'd taunted Alyssa in school, she'd vowed not to come back. Alyssa hung her head. Maybe if she'd visited more often she'd have noticed Grandmere's deterioration.

The door swung open, and her older sister pulled her into an embrace. "Alyssa! I was getting worried about you." CoCo's words warmed Alyssa as much as the hug.

Alyssa savored the bond. The connection she'd resisted for the past thirteen years felt…well, it felt good.

"Let me look at you." CoCo held her at arm's length. "You cut and colored your hair!"

Alyssa's hands automatically reached for the shorter-than-short hair on the back of her neck. "I had it highlighted."

"I like it," CoCo said with a nod. "Get in the house. You're soaked." She glanced down. "And why on earth are you barefoot?"

"Long story." Alyssa followed her sister into the house, her wet feet padding softly on the wooden floor, tracking mud with her steps. "Please tell me you have a pot of coffee on."

"Why don't you go upstairs and take a hot shower while I brew a fresh pot?"

"Sounds perfect." Alyssa paused, glancing around the living room. "Uh, where do you want me?"

"In your room, of course."

Her room. She didn't want a room to be considered hers. Not here.

Alyssa rolled her valise toward the staircase, then

hefted the strap over her shoulder. She trudged up the stairs—all sixteen of them—and halted at the landing. The door to the right stood ajar. Her younger sister's room. Alyssa stuck her head inside. Empty. She took a moment to hover in the doorway, drawing in the sweet smell of Tara's lingering perfume. With a grin, she turned and headed down the hall.

Frames filled with her mother's award-winning photos decorated the walls of the hallway. A knot tightened in Alyssa's stomach. She'd grown up seeing how high her mother had set the bar in journalistic endeavors. Wasn't that the reason she herself had gone into journalism—to honor her mother? Past CoCo's room, Alyssa stopped in front of the closed door. Her room.

Alyssa nudged open the door with her hip, and froze. Time had stood still. The room remained exactly as she'd left it. As if she'd never gone—as if the house waited for her homecoming. The hairs on the back of her neck rose to attention. Her vision dulled and a wave of nausea rose.

No! No more *cauchemars*. She'd suffered enough broken dreams in her life and didn't need them slamming her now.

She dropped her suitcase with a heavy *thunk*. Bending over, she retrieved clean clothes and her personal toiletries before marching into the hall to the bathroom. A hot shower would clear the cobwebs this house spun in her mind.

Fifteen minutes and a lot of vanilla-scented soap later, she bounded down the stairs and into the kitchen. CoCo stood at the stove, stirring a pot of aromatic gravy. She smiled as Alyssa shuffled in. "I thought you could use some biscuits and gravy."

"Smells wonderful." Her stomach rumbled in response. Loudly.

CoCo laughed. "Coffee's ready."

Alyssa poured herself a large mug of the dark brew and sniffed. The rich aroma with a hint of a woodsy scent… chicory. She mixed in plenty of sugar and stirred in the right amount of cream to make the cup qualify as a café au lait before she plunked into a kitchen chair. "Thanks for this. Where's Tara?"

Her sister set a plate of steaming biscuits and gravy in front of her, then sat across the table. "Working."

"Really? Where?" Taking a bite, Alyssa closed her eyes. She hadn't had chocolate gravy, cooked right, since…well, since Christmas morning three years ago. Her taste buds danced as the smooth thickness coated her tongue. A slice of heaven here on earth.

"Jazz club. She does their books at night."

"At least she's putting her degree to use. Finally."

The silence over the table hung as heavy as the rain outside.

"I didn't know for sure if you'd make the drive tonight." CoCo's eyes said what her words didn't.

Her sister had been afraid she wouldn't come at all. That said a lot about this sisterly bond thing.

"I told you when you called that I'd come."

"I'm just glad you're here, *Boo.*"

"Don't call me that."

"What?" Her sister had that wide-eyed, innocent look on her unblemished face.

"*Boo.*" Alyssa took a quick sip of coffee. "I don't like it."

CoCo jerked back as if she'd been slapped. "Oh. *Oui.*"

She wanted to tell CoCo not to talk Cajun at all, but

the hurt stomping across her sister's face made Alyssa hold her tongue.

"The storm sounds nasty."

As if on cue, thunder rumbled so loudly the kitchen window rattled. The sisters locked stares and joined in nervous laughs. The tension of the moment dissipated, if only briefly. Alyssa gazed out the window.

"Are you okay?"

She didn't like sharing her emotions. Never had. Ever since her parents died, she'd locked her pain and guilt inside. Alyssa glanced at her sister, nodded, paused, then shook her head. "Not really. I had an awful experience tonight."

"What happened?"

The image of the sheriff, cut and bleeding, lying in a plastic bag in the middle of a dirt road, slammed to the front of her mind. She shivered.

"What is it, Al?"

The menacing voice. The car driving off.

Alyssa pinched her eyes shut and shook her head. "I— I—"

His shallow breaths. The cuts. The swelling.

"Al? You're freaking me out here."

The rain mixing with blood. The strange but handsome friend.

CoCo gripped Alyssa's shoulder and shook. "Al!"

The motion jarred her back to the present. "I found Sheriff Theriot beaten near to death!"

"No way!"

An icy finger traced Alyssa's spine. She gripped the mug, begging its heat to warm her soul. She gulped in a deep breath and told her sister what had transpired.

The color drained from CoCo's face. Her features

tightened. "Oh, sweet mercy." She pulled Alyssa into a tight hug. "*Boo,* I'm so sorry this happened on your first night home."

This wasn't home, but Alyssa chose to keep her mouth shut, enjoying the hug too much. Only now did she feel the emptiness her decision to leave for good had created. Why hadn't she been able to bond with CoCo before?

CoCo released her, but kept an arm around her shoulders and drew her to her feet. "You need to get some rest. I'll call the hospital and Luc, too. He'll want to check on the sheriff."

Of course, CoCo's boyfriend would be good friends with the local lawman, while Alyssa didn't even have time for a love life. CoCo walked her toward the stairs, keeping up the stream of words. "We'll look in on him in the morning when we go to see Grandmere."

Alyssa came to a halt, jerking her sister when she stopped so quickly. "CoCo, I saw Grandmere before heading here. She looks really bad. What does her doctor say?"

"Just what I told you on the phone. She had a mild heart attack. They don't think there's any permanent damage but wanted to keep her a few days for observation, to make sure her oxygen levels stay up."

"She looks so…frail. So helpless."

"She *is* pushing seventy-three."

"But she didn't look this bad the last time I saw her."

CoCo pressed her lips together for a long moment. An array of emotions crossed her eyes—disappointment, regret, pain—but no condemnation. "Father Time has been catching up with her a bit faster these last few years, Al."

She should pack her bags—her sister had finalized the reservations for her guilt trip.

CoCo lowered her voice and gave her a half hug. "It's okay that you haven't been home in a while. Grandmere understands how important your career is to you."

Again, the reference to her career. Was it so wrong that she wanted to make something of herself? Away from this forsaken bayou? Alyssa stepped away. "If you would've told me she was bad off, I'd have come back."

"But she's been okay. Healthwise, anyway. Until this. I called as soon as the doctors told me."

"She's not okay, CoCo, and her condition didn't just happen overnight. She's had to have been going downhill for some time." She propped her hands on her hips, guilt putting a sassy edge to her words. "Are you blind to have not seen it?"

"Grandmere's getting older, that's all. The doctors will tell you she's healthy as a horse for a woman her age." CoCo laid a hand on her shoulder. "Everyone looks feeble in a hospital bed."

Alyssa shrugged free from her sister's touch. "That's something I want to talk to her doctor about tomorrow." She grabbed the tube of lip ointment from the pocket of her robe and glided the balm over the itchy scar. "Maybe we should take her to New Orleans. Or Shreveport. They have better doctors." She shoved the tube back into her pocket. She had to *do* something. That woman lying in the hospital wasn't the grandmother she remembered.

"The doctor here is fine. We'll talk to him in the morning."

"I have to be at the sheriff's station at eight-thirty."

"Whatever for?"

"To give my official statement about what I saw tonight."

"Oh, right. Why don't you get some sleep? We can look in on the sheriff in the morning, after you give your statement and before we visit Grandmere. Tara will go to the hospital as soon as she gets off work and stay with her until I get there in the morning."

Alyssa nodded and trudged up the stairs.

"Al?"

She stopped and glanced over her shoulder.

"I'm glad you're home."

This. Was. Not. Her. Home.

In the emergency room, the doctors and nurses hovered over Bubba. Jackson stood in the corner of the area, grateful they hadn't relegated him to the waiting room. His friend still hadn't regained consciousness. From what he could gather from the doctors' discussion, things weren't looking too positive for the sheriff. Jackson had caught the phrases "punctured lung," "broken ribs," "ocular damage," "broken nose" and "perforated kidney.' Not good, and Bubba still hadn't regained consciousness.

The attack was linked to the case. Nothing else made sense.

One of the machines hooked up to Bubba beeped and then squealed louder than the police scanner. A doctor jumped to press buttons while another pried open Bubba's swollen eyes and inspected with a little flashlight. Nurses bustled, handing confounding-looking instruments to the doctors. Suddenly, as if one, they moved Bubba's bed into the hall.

"Where are you taking him?" Jackson asked a nurse who rushed behind the group.

"Surgery," she called over her shoulder as she jogged to keep up.

Lord, please protect Bubba. He's a good man. A Christian. Guess I didn't need to tell You that, huh? Just watch over him, please, God.

Jackson ran a hand through his hair and shuffled to the waiting room. Maybe there'd be coffee available. It'd be bad, he knew, but nothing could be worse than the sludge he'd become accustomed to at the *Times-Picayune*. He maneuvered his way among the throng of activity in the emergency room. For such a small hospital, a lot happened. And the stench. Man, he hated the smell of hospitals, as if clouds of death and illness permeated the halls.

He recalled what Alyssa had said. Bubba pleading not to let someone get away with something. Using his name, obviously trying to give him a message. Two men hurrying before they were caught. What had she said about the car? Metallic blue Pontiac. Could he trust her impression? She hadn't seemed hysterical. Upset and shocked, yes, but hysterical and unreliable, no. As a journalist, she'd been trained to pick up on minute details. He reached into his back pocket and pulled out his Black-Berry. Within seconds he'd accessed the e-mail address for his friend at the New Orleans FBI office. He punched buttons.

NEED INFO ON ANY STOLEN BLUE PONTIACS IN VERMILION PARISH. ASAP. WILL EXPLAIN LATER.

He hesitated a moment, then he added one more sentence:

ALSO, ALL INFO YOU CAN FIND OUT ON AN ALYSSA LEBLANC. REPORTER IN SHREVEPORT. THANKS.

Once he sent the message, he turned off the Black-Berry and slipped the gadget back into his pocket. His thoughts were jumbled and he fought to organize them. While following up on a report of underage drinking, Bubba had found money dropped in the bayou—a payoff for something being smuggled. The sheriff had hooked Jackson up with a family friend, Frank Thibodeaux, to help him land a temporary job on the docks ten miles from Lagniappe. The local union allowed the intercoastal port to hire temporary workers at their own discretion. Jackson was scheduled to start work tonight. He glanced at his watch. Scheduled to start work in two hours, to be exact.

The hospital's automatic doors slid open with a whoosh. The splattering of rain against concrete echoed. Three uniformed deputies, including Gary Anderson, stomped inside. Their steps rang out sure and determined, and their wet soles squeaked against the linoleum floor.

"Deputy Anderson," Jackson called out.

"Mr. Devereaux." Gary strode toward him. The other officers trailed two steps behind. "How's the sheriff?"

"They took him to surgery."

"Surgery? For what?" one of the other deputies asked.

"I'm not sure. They just left a few minutes ago."

Deputy Anderson stared at him. "Did he say anything?"

"He never regained consciousness. That's really all I know." He hooked his thumb in his jeans pocket. "Anything come up with the case?"

Anderson huffed. "Guess you know the Feds will be here soon to take over. Assault on an officer of the law. I'm sure they'll want to talk to you in the morning. Why don't you plan on coming back by the station first thing tomorrow?"

A question sounding more like a directive.

One of the other lawmen cleared his throat. "We'll go check on the sheriff." He turned and headed for the nurses' station, the other man walking in perfect step alongside him.

Deputy Anderson tossed Jackson a steady look before joining the other two men.

Taking a sip of the tepid coffee, Jackson studied them. Yep, the FBI would rush in to take control. Their nosing around could hurt Jackson. He needed to be totally undercover on the docks to get to the truth. How would he handle the agents poking around?

Jackson Devereaux intended to find out exactly what was going on in Lagniappe.

Purpose dogging his every step, he hurried out into the rain to his truck. Bubba wouldn't want him to give up his undercover gig. Now more than ever, he needed answers.

The truck tires sang on the wet pavement as he cut through Lagniappe and hit the highway. Ten minutes and he'd be at the dock. He glanced in his rearview mirror. Between the rain and the stress, he looked the role of grunt laborer.

Jackson parked his truck and ambled to the dock. A bushy-bearded man a couple of inches shorter than

Jackson approached. "Can I help ya?" he hollered when Jackson reached the dock.

"Frank Thibodeaux recommended me for a temp job."

The man sidled up to Jackson. The stench of chewing tobacco filtered around him. "Doing what?"

"Loading and unloading. Anything for pay."

"Huh. Yeah, he mentioned it." The man's gaze drifted up and down Jackson, taking in his ratty jeans and hole-filled flannel shirt. He held out his hand. "Name's Burl. I'm the night foreman here."

Burl. Wow, did that name ever fit.

Jackson shook his hand. "Jax Delaney." Good thing he still had papers reflecting such a name. Who knew having an alias could come in handy so often?

"Ever done any dock work, Jax?"

"Yes, sir. Down in N'Awlins."

"Member of a union?"

"No, sir. I do scab work."

Burl nodded and passed him a pair of leather work gloves. "Let's go ahead and get ya to work. If ya do a good job, I'll put ya on the payroll tomorrow."

"Yes, sir." Jackson gripped the coarse gloves. Too bad he didn't have to fill out paperwork before being put on the dock. He'd been counting on that. Oh, well. Go with it.

But he'd keep his eyes open for when opportunity knocked.

THREE

Harsh lights. Beeps. Voices.

Her heart raced. Oh, the sting. The pain.

The tears ran down her cheeks. Someone swiped them away with a rough cloth. Her face burned, especially just below her lip.

Scorching. White-hot throbbing.

A doctor prying her eyes open to shine a light in them. Bright, too bright. His voice calm, soothing, asking her if she remembered the wreck.

The crash.

Momee! Papa!

Alyssa sat upright, the sheet twisted into a tight wad at her feet. Another nightmare. She shook her head. It'd been years since she'd had one. Three, to be exact—the last time she'd visited. Just being in Lagniappe brought her nightmares back full force.

The bayou's chief export was pain. Always had been, always would be.

Alyssa moved to the bedroom window and watched the wind rip dried leaves from the limbs. The storm had passed through the night, escorting in a cold front. Alyssa shook her head. Yeah, right. A cold front in Lagniappe?

Not hardly. Then again, she'd have said there weren't any attractive, good men here, either. Well, aside from her sister's boyfriend.

The image of that handsome man, Jackson Devereaux, kept flittering to her mind. His kindness in pulling her car out of the ditch. So courteous, despite wanting to go check on his friend. His image refused to be banished from her mind. Just as it had for the majority of the night, making her sleep restless and putting her in a cranky mood. Probably partially causing her nightmare.

Where had she seen him before?

Movement on the bank of the bayou caught her attention. CoCo in her airboat, checking on her beloved alligators. Why her sister wasted a good college education studying the prehistoric reptiles was beyond her realm of comprehension. Didn't CoCo see the bayou would forever be doomed?

Alyssa turned from the window, letting the pink curtains drift back into place. The lacy things she'd picked out at the tender age of fourteen. Her heart hiccuped.

She lifted the picture sitting on her bedside table. Her parents. Oh, how she longed for them to be with her today. Her mother, always on an assignment with the newspaper, had a camera looped around her neck. Would Alyssa ever measure up to her mother's expectations? Standing beside Momee in the picture, her father smiled down at his wife with love and adoration in his eyes. Could Alyssa ever find someone who'd look at her like that?

Oh, I miss you both so much.

Tears filled her eyes. She blinked several times, refusing to go down the path of her past. Not today. She had to move forward. But here, where memories assaulted her every moment? At least in Shreveport she had a life—a promising career, a nice apartment, a normal church life. Lagniappe offered her nothing but the memories of how much she'd lost—her parents, her childhood, all sense of normalcy.

She grabbed her sneakers and slipped them over her socks. Fastening on her watch, she noted the time. Lovely. She'd barely have time to chug a cup of coffee before she had to go to the sheriff's office. At least she could smell the strong java.

A half pot awaited her in the empty kitchen. Without Grandmere and her sisters, the house was entirely too quiet. Too still. As if holding its breath in anticipation of something. Alyssa's heartbeat quickened. She jerked the glass pot free from the warmer and poured a cup. Her hands trembled. Coffee splashed onto her hand. She jumped, hitting the carafe against the porcelain sink. The pot shattered with a loud crash. Glass and coffee spilled into the sink, on the counter and onto the floor.

Couldn't anything go right?

The blame lay with the bayou. Didn't everything? When her parents had died and she'd been forced to leave New Orleans, her family's involvement in voodoo had given her schoolmates every reason in the world to hate her. To ridicule her, to torment her every school day. Now she could even smell the destruction in the air, lurking to wreak havoc in her life again. But she'd matured, wised up. The bayou wouldn't beat her down this time. Alyssa stiffened her spine and went about passing a mop.

The front door slammed. Alyssa tossed the dish towel into the open washer before CoCo called out, "Al?"

Alyssa gritted her teeth against the nickname. Better

than *Boo* at least. If only she could make her sister understand Cajun wasn't a real language—only a mix of several different ones.

CoCo cleared the kitchen threshold, her long curls held captive by a ponytail at the nape of her neck. "Good, you're up."

Why not just state the obvious? "Of course, I'm up. I have to be at the station in twenty minutes." She felt as if her nerves rested outside her body.

"I know. Listen, I'm going straight to the hospital to relieve Tara." CoCo studied Alyssa. "Unless you want me to go with you?"

"No. It shouldn't take long to give my statement. I'll meet you at the hospital."

"Okay." CoCo moved to the counter as Alyssa swung her purse over her shoulder and strode toward the door. "Where's the coffeepot?"

Alyssa chuckled under her breath and escaped the confines of the house. Wind tickled her long bangs against her forehead. Leaves danced on the breeze, twisting and turning and carrying the scent of the bayou. The stench. Alyssa ducked into her car as quickly as possible.

The torrential downpour had made the roads so muddy that going more than twenty miles per hour could ditch a car faster than greased lightning—like last night. Alyssa parked the car, straightened her shoulders and strode into the building nearly covered with kudzu.

Chaos had taken over the sheriff's office. Phones rang unanswered, several men dressed in jeans milled about, and the odor of burnt coffee hovered in the air. Alyssa stood in the waiting area, staring at the unmanned counter.

No one addressed her—they didn't even seem to be aware she'd entered.

"Excuse me."

No one even bothered to look up.

The scar under her lip burned. Shaking off the memory, she reached for her lip balm. She applied the balm, stuck the tube back into her pocket, cleared her throat and hollered louder.

A platinum-haired woman stuck her head around the door next to the counter. "I'm sorry, hang on a second." A moment passed before she faced Alyssa, popping her gum. "How can we help you?"

"My name is Alyssa LeBlanc and I was to—"

The woman's eyes widened. "You're the one who found Bubba?"

"Well, yes."

"*Merci,* ma'am. You probably saved his life." She dabbed at her face with red-tipped nails. "Just a minute." The woman didn't take a step away from the counter, just turned and shrieked to the room at large. "Hey, the woman who found Bubba is here."

Every head turned to stare at her as if she'd sprouted a third eye, and all activity ceased. Only the constant shrill of the phone remained.

Time transported Alyssa back to high school, when she'd been stared at before. To the girls' bathroom.

She washed her hands, the water lukewarm. Three cheer-leaders came in, took notice of her, stared and laughed.

"Ooh, get a load of that outfit."

"Is that your sister's old jacket, or did you get that wearable patchwork quilt at the consignment shop?"

The head cheerleader smirked. "Y'all had better be

nice. Don't ya know—her grandmother's the voodoo queen. She'll cast a spell on you."

"Or her sister."

Their taunting continued to ring in her ears. Alyssa swallowed and blinked slowly.

Would someone please answer the phone?

The room shifted.

No! Not here, not now. No daymares, please. Alyssa grabbed the counter and braced herself.

As if someone threw a switch, everyone snapped out of their trance. Phones were answered, voices rose above the hum of machines. Two men in black suits approached her.

"Ms. LeBlanc?" The man was handsome, tanned, fit and wearing an interested look.

She didn't reply. She couldn't be sure she wouldn't zone out.

"I'm Agent Lockwood with the FBI." He flashed a smile sure to weaken some women's knees.

The room righted itself. Good. She released her grip on the grooved counter. "Mr. Lockwood." She gave a slight nod, aware of her tenuous hold on her equilibrium.

He motioned to the bald man standing beside him. "This is Agent Ward."

She acknowledged Agent Ward before focusing her attention back to the handsome Lockwood. "A deputy told me last night to come in and give my statement."

"Yes, ma'am. Come on back." He held open the little swinging door attached to the counter. Southern manners at their best, yet the agent hadn't spoken with an accent.

She followed him into the large area, then down a hall and into an interrogation room. He waved toward the table. "Please, have a seat."

As she settled in the hardback chair, she studied the young agent from beneath lowered lashes. Short, dark hair. A trimmed goatee. Not too tall, but not short. Trim and muscular. What some women would call a catch. But something in his eyes caught Alyssa's attention. An arrogance…a lurking deception. She decided she didn't like him.

Turning her attention to the other agent, Ward, she noticed the lines etched deep into his face. Older than his partner but, as she scrutinized his eyes, not wiser. He, too, had something about him that blared untrustworthiness. She didn't care for him, either.

"Ms. LeBlanc, we have the notes from Deputy Anderson, but if you wouldn't mind, would you please give us a recounting of what transpired last night?" He pushed a button on a digital recorder and laid the small gadget on the table. "We tape this to make sure we're accurate in your statement."

Yeah, right. She used recorders constantly in interviews, mostly to trap someone in a lie. Still, the quicker she got this done, the sooner she could leave. Alyssa took a deep breath and retold what had happened the previous night.

The agents took notes as she spoke. Good interview habits—she did the same thing herself.

"Did you recognize the men?" Agent Lockwood asked.

"No, I couldn't see them clearly. Just figures and voices."

"Would you recognize their voices?"

The one who'd said to hurry, she'd never forget his. Even now the memory of the deep timbre gave her the heebie-jeebies. "One of them. The other, maybe." She ran her finger over the burning under her lip and lifted her shoulder—casually, she hoped.

"Now, can you elaborate on what Sheriff Theriot said to you?"

"Only what I've already told you. I know nothing more than that." Were they dense, or trying to see if she would lie? Why would she? She didn't even live here, much less know what the sheriff had meant. She only recognized him because he'd just been elected sheriff when she'd last visited.

"I'm sure you understand assault of a police officer is a federal offense. A felony," Lockwood said.

Did she really care whose jurisdiction the case fell under?

"You're the only material witness," Ward interjected. "An eyewitness."

An eerie sensation washed over in waves. Sweat lined her palms.

"Until we know more, we'll have to ask you not to leave town for the time being."

"What?" *No!* The urge to scream rose in her throat. She bit the inside of her throbbing lip. "I have a job in Shreveport I have to get back to." Her voice quivered, but she didn't care. She couldn't stay here. She'd had enough experience with government officials to know their process could take a mighty long time. Something she didn't have a lot of—not if she didn't want to lose her place at the paper. Or her sanity.

"I'm sure your editor will understand. Hopefully, it'll only be for a couple more days." Lockwood flashed that disarming smile of his. "If we bring a suspect in for questioning, we might have to put them in a lineup to see if you can pick out the voice."

She couldn't stay here—she'd run as far and as fast from her past as she could when she'd left. Alyssa balled her hands into tight fists, the urge to hit something powerful. Right now, Special Agent Smiley looked like a pretty good target. "I can't stay here."

"I'm sorry, ma'am, but we can't let you leave yet," Agent Baldy said.

"You can't make me stay." She jerked to her feet, the chair scraping against the battered linoleum floor.

Lockwood stood as well, only more dignified. "Actually, we can. We could place you in custody."

"But we'd rather you stayed because you know it's the right thing to do," Ward said.

Red hot anger coursed through her veins. Her heart thudded so hard her ribs hurt. "Fine. For how long?"

"Until we can get this case wrapped up."

"How long do you think that'll be?" She clenched and unclenched her hands.

"It all depends." The light reflected off his bald head, casting a glare around him. A dark blue infused the light.

"Are you okay, Ms. LeBlanc?"

She glared at Lockwood. "I'm fine. I just don't want to be here."

"We understand," Ward started.

Alyssa held up her hand toward Agent Ward, but focused on Lockwood. "Just hurry up and do your job so I can get out of here."

Jackson took quick steps toward the sheriff's office. His mission—find out everything he could about the money dropped in the bayou and see who else Bubba might've told. Everything Bubba shared with him about the incident, the location of the money drop and the tag on the bag, stank of drug trafficking—he'd reported on it countless times back in New Orleans. But here in La-gniappe? Then again, there was the intercoastal port. Would make smuggling easier. Too bad he'd only moved around sealed crates last night on the docks.

His mind already flipping through his mental Rolodex, Jackson kept marching toward the police station. A breeze stirred the air, carrying the clear smell of wet soil. Just as he reached for the handle, the door swung open, nearly slamming against him. He jumped back onto the sidewalk and opened his mouth to speak when he noticed who'd nearly knocked him on his can.

Alyssa LeBlanc. And from the look on her face, she wasn't a happy camper.

"Good morning, Ms. LeBlanc."

She jerked her gaze to meet his. The anger slipped from her eyes. "Oh. Mr. Devereaux."

Hey, she remembered his name despite the circumstances of last night. Bonus points. "How're you this morning, *chère?*"

Her eyes darkened, the green rings around the irises flashing under the morning sun. "Not so good."

"What's wrong? Have they uncovered something about the case?"

"No. That's the problem." She crossed her arms over her chest.

Uh-oh. Pure defensive body language.

He risked taking a step closer. "I understand. It's frustrating to see Bubba like that and not have a clue who's behind it."

"Those imbeciles won't figure out a thing." She met his stare. "How's the sheriff?"

"I talked to the nurses before I headed here. They said

he had a rough night. Came out of surgery okay, but he's in a coma."

Softness seeped into the edges of her eyes. "I'm so sorry. I'll stop by and look in on him."

This woman was an enigma. Strong and steady in a crisis, yet emotional about people. What a rare combination. One that pushed his heart rate up a notch or two. He owed it to Bubba to concentrate on the case at hand. He couldn't afford distractions, no matter how attractive. "I guess I'll see you later then, *chère*. I've got to go answer more questions."

A strange expression clouded her delicate features for a fraction of a second before she straightened her shoulders. "Good luck with that. Hope you have a good day, Mr. Devereaux." She marched toward her dirty Honda.

"Jackson."

Pivoting, she tossed him a puzzled look. "Excuse me?"

"Jackson. It's my name."

"Oh." She spun around and opened her car door. "Good day, Mr. Devereaux."

He watched her drive away, her spunk giving him a charge. He'd bet his bottom dollar she'd earned her stripes as a reporter. Oh, not as good as him, but good nonetheless. With a chuckle, he headed into the sheriff's office.

Missy, the dispatcher with that bright yellow-blond hair, stood behind the counter. He knew she'd broken the thirty-year mark recently, but the lines in her face told of a harder-than-normal life. Her eyes lit as he approached. "Well, well, well, Mr. Devereaux. How are you?"

Her attraction came across too obviously for Jackson's liking. Not at all like the elusive Alyssa LeBlanc. He smiled easily. "Been a long night." With no sleep. "I'm supposed to answer more questions this morning."

"Let me call the agents for you." She smiled knowingly as she lifted the receiver, spoke in whispers and replaced the phone. "Go on back to the conference room."

He nodded his thanks and pushed through the swinging door. So many people milled about. Off-duty officers called in to help, or new eyes brought in to work the case. He skidded to a stop at the interrogation room.

Two suits, screaming standard-issue agent, hovered around the doorway. "Mr. Devereaux?" the young man with the knot of his tie pressed against his Adam's apple asked. "I'm Agent Lockwood with the FBI. This is Agent Ward."

No big shocker. Suits, no personality, same neutral expression—of course they were FBI agents. He'd have to play nice to get the info he needed. Mustering a fake smile, he extended his hand. "Morning, gentlemen."

Agent Lockwood escorted him into the interrogation room, gave the basic introductions, then recorded his account of last night's events with his digital recorder. Pretty much same old, same old for Jackson's line of work.

"Why, exactly, are you visiting Sheriff Theriot?" Agent Ward asked, his bald head resembling an egg.

Ah, now they were getting there—the big questions. "We're old frat buddies. We hadn't seen each other in several months, so when Bubba called and invited me, I came." Jackson leaned the chair back on two legs and met the agents' stares head-on. Let the games begin.

"Isn't that a bit difficult for you? Being a big-shot reporter and all?" Lockwood took over the questioning.

"Not really. There was nothing pressing in N'Awlins, and a change sounded like fun."

"Coming to Lagniappe?"

Jackson smiled. They wouldn't trip him up. "Visiting my friend sounded like fun."

"I see. You arrived in town when?" Agent Ward hunched over his notebook.

"Wednesday."

"How long are you staying?"

"Well, we didn't exactly say, but now…I intend to stay until Bubba's better." He plopped the chair down to all fours. "And until the culprit is apprehended, of course."

Lockwood and Ward exchanged a quick glance. These two obviously hadn't been in the field long—standard rule of the federal boys: don't communicate in any manner in front of an interviewee. Jackson refrained from shaking his head. Alyssa had been right. The agents didn't instill confidence in their crime-solving abilities.

"Why would the sheriff invite you to visit, Mr. Devereaux?" Agent Lockwood asked.

Finally, they asked the right question. Too bad they wouldn't get the right answer. "Maybe he was lonely. He called and invited me. I came. That's it."

Lockwood all but sneered. "Sure seems your timing is impeccable, Mr. Devereaux. You're here not even a week, and someone viciously attacks the friend you're visiting."

"You were the first to arrive on the scene after the report of the incident," interjected Ward. "Before the police and medical personnel could get there."

"And Bubba said my name before he lost consciousness." They were wasting time. Valuable time. "I'm sure it'd be neat and tidy to put me at the top of the suspect list, but you're barking up the wrong tree, boys." Jackson stood and pushed his chair under the table. "Bubba is my friend. I'm staying at his house. If I wanted to hurt him, do you think I'd beat him within an inch of his life and then leave him in the middle of a road? Puh-leeze. Think about it—I got there first because I heard the dispatcher's report over Bubba's scanner."

"The sheriff just happened to mention your name when he told Ms. LeBlanc not to let them get away with it." Ward stood, pocketing his notebook. "Care to explain that?"

"Maybe he wanted someone to call me. Let me know." They'd waste time investigating him. Sure, it looked off to them, but if they had an ounce of good detecting skills, they'd have already ruled him out as a suspect.

"Uh-huh." Agent Ward glared at him. "Guess it goes without saying that you need to stay in town."

"Like I said, I have no intention of going anywhere until I know my friend is okay." Jackson jammed his thumb into his pocket and turned toward the door. "Now, if that's all, I want to get to the hospital to check on Bubba."

And follow up on some leads, since the men in black appeared to be what Alyssa had called them—imbeciles.

FOUR

She could slam a revolving door right now.

Alyssa fumed in the hospital parking lot, grasping her cell phone in a death grip. She smacked the side of her fist against the steering wheel. How could she call her editor and tell him she'd be stuck in stupid Lagniappe until the stupid cops solved an attempted murder case? She'd lose all she'd been working so hard for. So not fair. She'd done the right thing, and now she'd be penalized. Where was the justice?

Knowing she couldn't prolong the agony anymore, she punched the speed-dial button for Simon's cell. One ring. Two.

"Simon Woods."

"Hey, boss. It's Alyssa."

"How's your grandma?"

"She's okay. Looks weaker than I remember." She glanced at her watch and grimaced. "The doctor should be making rounds soon."

"Great. I've managed to hold off giving your assignment to Marlee since you'll be back in a couple of days." His deep laugh resonated in her ear. "She wasn't exactly thrilled, either."

Alyssa could imagine. For the past several months, the aggressive up-and-coming reporter nipped at Alyssa's heels, waiting to swoop in and steal Alyssa's prime assignments. Repressed sobs burned in her chest. Marlee would get her chance. "About that…"

"Don't tell me."

"It can't be helped. I'm an eyewitness in a federal felony case, and the Feds won't let me leave town." The tears made tracks down her cheeks as she eased the lip balm from her pocket.

"You're kidding, right?"

No, I'm making it up just to annoy you. "I wish I were."

"Can they do that?"

"They're the FBI—they can pretty much do whatever they want."

The silence over the line prophesied the death of her career.

"Guess them's the breaks, kid." Simon's voice held a hint of irritation.

I'm fine, thank you for asking. Don't worry for a second I might be a target for the bad guys, but hey, that's no big deal, right? "It's not like I want to stay here. You know I hate this place."

"Well, you gotta do what you gotta do."

"I know." She gripped the steering wheel tightly. "Maybe I can cover this crime for our paper."

"What happened?"

"Assault on the sheriff." Did he miss the part where she'd said she was an eyewitness?

"Too local. Not of interest to our readers."

Dismay mixed with frustration threatened to suffocate her even more than Lagniappe. "I see."

"Hey, I know." Simon's tone went upbeat. "Cover the politics in that neck of the woods. Heard there's a hot Senate race in that district—someone daring to run against the incumbent of, like, twenty years or something. Maybe you can dig up some dirt. Scoop those locals down there. We all know you're better than those small-time reporters."

His compliment did little to soothe the knot in her chest. And his concern for her well-being was touching, just touching. She swallowed her irritation. "Sure. I'm on it."

"The incumbent's name is…" Papers rustled over the connection. "Edmond Mouton."

She blinked several times as her heart caught. It'd been a long time since she'd heard the name. Her parents' funeral, to be exact.

"Alyssa? You there?"

"Uh, yeah. I know Mr. Mouton. Well, I did."

"Even better. Get to digging, girl."

"I'll get right to it. Thanks, boss."

He broke the connection without saying goodbye. Typical Simon. She dropped the cell phone into her purse.

Edmond Mouton. He'd been a friend of her mother's, granting Claire LeBlanc access he denied other photojournalists. Some of those liberties won her awards. No one had run against Mouton for his Senate seat in a decade and a half. Maybe she could use her mother's connection to get an exclusive with him. He could jumpstart her career as he'd done her mother's.

A load lifted off Alyssa's shoulders as she strode toward the hospital. Things might be looking up after all. She checked her watch again and quickened her steps, not wanting to miss the doctor.

Alyssa let out a breath and marched into the hospital, her steps stronger than she felt. She nodded at the nurses as she passed their station before sweeping into her grandmother's room.

CoCo sat in the chair, reading the paper aloud to Grandmere. Her grandmother glanced up. "Alyssa, *ma chère,* how're you this morning?"

"I'm okay." Alyssa kissed her grandmother's cheek. "The question is, how are you?"

Grandmere's eyes twinkled, although weighted down with wrinkles. Some of the color had returned to her face—she didn't appear nearly as pale and pasty as before. "I'm fine, just like I told you last night."

"Has the doctor been by yet?"

"You just missed him." CoCo laid the paper on the bedside tray and stood, raising her arms in a stretch. "He said if all went well, Grandmere can come home tomorrow afternoon. Isn't that wonderful?"

"I told y'all I'd just had an episode. Nothing to fret about." Grandmere's gaze darted back and forth between CoCo and Alyssa. "How're you two getting along?"

Leave it to their grandmother to cut right to the chase.

"We're fine, Grandmere." CoCo grinned across the bed. "Right, Al?"

Alyssa nodded. "We're good."

"I sense something. What aren't you telling me?" Grandmere squeezed Alyssa's hand.

"Don't be silly, Grandmere." CoCo's voice quivered with tension.

But their grandmother wasn't fooled. She narrowed her eyes as she studied Alyssa and squeezed her hand harder. "Alyssa, what's wrong with you?"

Alyssa caught CoCo's warning look, but shook her head. "Grandmere, someone beat Sheriff Theriot last night and left him for dead in the middle of the road." She tightened her hold on her grandmother's hand. "I found him and called for help. He's here. In a coma."

"Mercy, child. The spirits warned me something wasn't right."

The spirits told her? Yeah, right.

"Grandmere," CoCo said with gentle chiding. "I've told you—"

"*Oui,* child, you've told me. You believe your way, I'll believe mine."

For once, the sisters were on the same side of an issue. Heat seeped through Alyssa. At least they had something in common. "Where's Tara?"

"Went home to sleep. The child doesn't need to be up here babysitting me after working." Grandmere threw CoCo a hard stare.

"She wants to come, Grandmere. Let us fuss over you, will ya?" CoCo's smile held such love and concern that Alyssa had to look away.

Would she ever fit in here? With her own family?

Alyssa withdrew her hand. "I'm going to check on the sheriff."

"Luc looked in on him earlier. He's still in a coma," CoCo said.

"I'll be back in a bit." Alyssa kissed Grandmere's temple. "You behave yourself," she whispered.

Grandmere chuckled.

Alyssa stopped at the nurses' station to find out where they'd taken the sheriff. Fourth floor. Another trial to endure—the elevator. Small, confining metal car…she could almost smell the burning gasoline. She held her breath as she counted the numbers flashing over the door of the elevator. She rubbed her lip and forced herself to keep her eyes open. She had to fight the memories—they were always stronger in Lagniappe. The car finally dinged at four, and the doors eased open. She couldn't get out fast enough.

And immediately wished she could run back.

The odor of sickness hovered in the hallway, as if waiting to jump inside some healthy person when he least expected it. Alyssa shuddered. Hospitals always evoked memories. Bad memories. The ones that led to *cauchemars*.

No more dreams. Not after the one last night.

She let out a pent-up breath and headed toward the sheriff's room. She'd arrived at the ICU before it dawned on her she'd slipped back into Cajun. While annoyed, she understood her error. Being around both CoCo and Grandmere almost guaranteed the use of the language. She'd be more careful now. Pay closer attention to her feelings.

Alyssa approached the ICU nurses' station. "Excuse me. I'd like to check on Sheriff Theriot."

A middle-aged nurse glanced at her from behind lowered glasses. "The sheriff isn't allowed but one visitor at a time, and his friend is in with him now." She jutted her chin toward a room with nothing but a glass wall. "But you can look at him from the observation window there."

"Thank you." Alyssa moved toward the glass, her heartbeat warring with the sounds of beeps and dings from all the medical equipment. She gripped the rail in front of the window, and her heart caught.

Jackson Devereaux sat in the chair next to the bed, holding a Bible. His lips moved as his fingers kept place in the Scriptures. She didn't want to be impressed, but couldn't help but be mesmerized. A man, reading the Bible aloud to a friend in a coma? Alyssa had never seen anyone, save the preacher of her church back home, read the Bible, much less read aloud. Interesting.

"…but the greatest of these is love." Jackson looked up from 1 Corinthians 13:13 as he caught movement out of the corner of his eye, his heart thrumming. Heat crept up his neck. Slowly he turned to face the glass wall.

And met Alyssa LeBlanc's stare.

He smiled at her, closed the Bible and set the book on the little table beside Bubba. "I'm going to see this lady, Bubba." He patted his friend's shoulder. "I keep running into her and now she's here, just as I read about love. Gotta wonder if God's trying to tell me something." He straightened and headed to the door.

"I didn't mean to interrupt you." Something guarded darted across her eyes. "I only came by to check on the sheriff."

"I just finished. I needed some water anyway."

"Oh. I didn't mean to intrude."

"Don't be silly, *chère*. You're no interruption." He tucked his thumb in his jeans pocket and studied her. "Would you like to join me for a quick bite?"

She glanced at her watch. "I need to check back with my grandmother."

Everything inside him propelled him to be insistent. Something about this woman called out to him. "There's a sandwich shop across the street. Won't take but a few minutes." He noticed the battle in her facial expression. "There are a couple of things I'd like to discuss with you. Why someone would attack Bubba, for starters."

Since when did he all but bribe a woman to go out with him?

"All right, I guess."

He fought to keep his smile cordial, not let it expand into the grin rising from his chest. Jackson offered her his arm. "Milady."

Her soft touch near his wrist sent his pulse spiking as they headed to the elevators. What was wrong with him? Not many women caused such a reaction. Must be because he was distraught over Bubba. That had to be the reason.

As they waited for the elevator car to arrive, her grip on his arm tightened. He studied her from the corner of his eye. She paled under the harsh lights. Her lips were pressed tightly together, making her high cheekbones even more prominent. He noticed a small red circle right under her lip, something he'd never seen before. A birthmark? Still, a striking woman. But one who'd suddenly become quite uncomfortable. "Something wrong?"

She jerked her gaze to his face. "What?"

"You're tensing up. Is something wrong?"

"Oh. I'm just not fond of elevators."

The doors slid open.

"Would you rather take the stairs?"

"No, thank you. I'm okay." As if to prove her point, she marched into the car.

He grinned and followed. "Claustrophobic?"

"Something like that. So, tell me how the sheriff's doing."

Good change of subject. Smooth. He had to give her points. "He's about the same. Still in a coma. They found two bullets in his stomach when they performed his surgery."

"He'd been shot?"

"Shot twice, stabbed eight times and beaten with a hard, blunt object." He led her from the elevator. "It's a miracle he's still alive and that his major organs weren't damaged more than they are."

"Mercy sakes alive! I had no idea."

"Wish I knew who did this to him." Jackson escorted her out of the hospital and onto the sidewalk. "I mean, Bubba's a really likeable person. The attack has to be linked to a case."

She arched a smooth eyebrow. "Did Bert and Ernie tell you anything this morning?"

"Who?"

She laughed, the sound surprisingly light and airy. "I'm sorry. I was referring to the two FBI agents at the station."

He paused, puzzled. Then it dawned on him. *Sesame Street.* He let out a loud laugh. "Good comparison." Jackson held her elbow as they moved to the crosswalk. "No, they didn't tell me anything. Matter of fact, they treated me as the main suspect. I'm concerned they won't even bother looking for the real attackers."

"Why do you think they won't investigate thoroughly?" Her question appeared innocent enough, but Jackson caught the hesitant tone.

"Mainly because I'm an outsider here. I'm an easy suspect. Bubba did say my name."

"Oh." She kept walking toward the sandwich place.

"Small town people are normally leery of outsiders."

"But the agents aren't from here, either."

"True." Yet he'd gotten the impression the agents wanted to close the case quickly, even if that meant blaming the wrong guy.

"Where are you from?" she asked.

"N'Awlins."

He opened the door and let her precede him into the shop. The enticing aroma of grilled onions and peppers filled the small space. His stomach rumbled as they wove around tables for two to the counter. They ordered dressed po'boys and colas. The cashier took his money, gave him change and a ticket number, and told them to have a seat. They found a vacant table shoved up against the window.

"New Orleans? I'm from there," she continued the conversation once they sat down.

"Really? I don't hear the accent, *chère*. Besides, I thought you were born and raised in Lagniappe."

"Not hardly."

"But, I th—"

She shook her head. "My parents were killed in a car accident when I was fourteen. My sisters and I were brought here to live with our grandparents." She blinked away tears. "But I moved as soon as I graduated."

The distaste came across clear in her voice. He tried to imagine her scenario—on the cusp of womanhood and losing your parents, then being yanked from a big city into a little bumpkin town. Yeah, he could understand her displeasure with Lagniappe. "Where'd you go to college?"

"LSU."

"Go Tigers, eh?"

"All the way, baby." She grinned, her eyes twinkling.

The girl behind the counter called their number, and he retrieved their tray. Alyssa reached for one of the sodas, while he separated the wrapped sandwiches and handed one to her. She removed the paper, lifted the bread and doused the meat liberally with pepper.

"Ah, but you eat like a true native."

She laughed as she set down the shaker.

"Would you like me to pray?"

Her smile vanished. "Uh, okay."

That answered his question from last night—her use of the word *praying* had merely been a phrase. He hated the disappointment filling his chest, but ducked his head and offered up grace.

Alyssa ate with relish. He tried to keep up an ongoing conversation, but his heart beat cold.

Why, God, did You make me feel there was something special about this one, only to let me find out she's not really following You?

A Scripture flickered across his mind. He couldn't recall the line in its entirety at the moment, nor the chapter and verse, but he recognized it from Kings. And he sure knew why he'd recalled this particular Scripture at this moment.

For You alone know the hearts of men.

God had a reason for placing this particular woman on his path time and again. Jackson's job would be to figure out what the Lord wanted him to do about her.

FIVE

"So, what did you want to tell me?" Alyssa took a final pull of her soft drink and stared at Jackson amid the crowded sandwich shop. She marveled at herself—when had she begun to think of him on a first-name basis? What had happened to her initial feeling of dislike?

He wiped his mouth with the napkin before squishing the paper into a tight wad and dropping it onto the tray. "You're a reporter, yes?"

"Right." On the road to becoming the best, if she could ever get out of this hick town.

"Have you ever worked on a story involving a federal government investigation?"

"One or two." Only white collar crimes, and only as a backup reporter, but he didn't need to know the details.

He glanced around the small shop, his gaze lighting on the patrons closest to their table, and lowered his voice. "Then you know they aren't always after the truth, but just getting a conviction."

Words failed her, which was pretty sad considering how she made her living. Her mind recalled several stories she'd helped research about the corruption of officers and how their supervisors demanded a high percent of convictions in their cases. The *Shreveport Times* had run a front page article, exposing the frauds, not even six months ago. "Yeah, I've seen that."

"It's very likely the FBI will focus on me and my presence here, and let the real attackers get away, despite Deputy Anderson's report to the contrary. Already over twelve hours have passed since you found Bubba. You know as well as I do that the first twenty-four hours are the most critical."

He looked so earnest, so sincere. Why would he try to convince her, of all people, and not the police? She didn't carry any weight in this town. Yet everything he'd said made perfect sense, and her gut instinct told her to trust him.

"Mr. Devereaux, I don't know you. Why are you telling me all this?"'"

"Because you're a reporter, and I think once you hear what I have to tell you, your gut instinct will be to dig for the truth."

She considered that for a moment before nodding. "Go ahead."

"I'm going to take a chance and tell you what I know. Bubba'd been investigating a case, something just starting up, and he'd gotten stonewalled. He called me to come see what I could uncover. That's the reason I'm here in town."

A wave of excitement surged within her. "What kind of case?"

His gaze locked onto her eyes, as if reading her intentions.

She sighed. "Look, you asked me to help, you trusted me enough to tell me what you already have. Just spill it."

"Bubba found a couple of money drops in the bayou."

"What, exactly, does that mean?"

"A bag of money, sealed in a plastic bag, is tied to a

small buoy. Someone drops the money into the water, normally from a plane flying under radar. The pick-up person comes by later and grabs the bag."

"Isn't that normally done in drug trafficking?"

"Yes." He pulled the lid from his cup and crunched on ice.

"Hard to believe drug deals would be happening in Lagniappe."

"The town does have a lot of voodoo, which oft times involves drugs."

She sucked in air through her teeth and tried to evoke the memories she'd suppressed for so many years. Her grandmother had never condoned use of any drugs in any of her ceremonies or rites, as far as she knew. "Drugs aren't always involved in voodoo stuff."

"No, not always. Something else you have to re-member—the intercoastal ports are only ten or so miles away. Easy access to move the drugs, which would make the money drops in the bayou logical."

Alyssa tapped a finger against her chin, rolling ideas around in her mind. "We pretty much can figure the ship-ments are going out of the intercoastal port." This could be a great story. Something big enough that Simon wouldn't consider the subject local and of no interest to the rest of the state—something that would mean her time here wasn't a total waste. Alyssa tried to mask her excitement by forcing her voice to remain even. "What did the sheriff discover in his investigation?"

"Bubba tried running some leads, but each way he went, he hit a dead end."

Alyssa thought of all the articles she'd studied and assisted in researching. Oh, yeah, this could be huge. "To have the power to stop a police investigation normally means someone of importance is involved."

"Right. That's exactly what Bubba thought, which is why he called me and asked me to help. I've been doing a little undercover investigation."

She didn't like the gleam in his eye, screaming trouble. "What?"

"I'm doing some temporary grunt work down at the intercoastal port."

If he exposed where the drugs were going, he'd put himself right in the line of fire. Wait a minute. Why did she care? She shouldn't, but the thought of him in danger…

"I don't think that's such a good idea. I mean, it could be months before you find out something useful."

"Not if I'm determined to snoop, as I am." The cockiness in his tone left no argument.

"What if you're exposed?"

"*Chère,* Bubba set me up with someone already working on the dock who hadn't a clue about any drug smuggling but was all too happy to help out. The night foreman, Burl, has already tried me out." He smiled that easygoing, disarming smile of his. "Don't worry, I'm good at digging out the truth."

She stared hard at him as another thought slammed her—she hadn't a clue what Jackson did for a living and why the sheriff would be inclined to call him for help on a case. "Are you in law enforcement?"

He chuckled. "Not hardly. I'm a reporter."

New Orleans. Reporter.

Why hadn't she trusted her gut instinct about not liking him? Why hadn't she made the time to Google him as she'd intended? Her breath froze in her lungs. "What paper?"

Don't say it, don't say it, don't say it.

"The *Times-Picayune*."

She felt as if swamp water flooded her heart.

"Alyssa?"

She studied him. The eyes that had so mesmerized her were what had made her sense she'd seen him before. Could he be? No, surely not.

"How long have you worked for the *Times-Picayune?*"

"About five years, but was promoted to investigative reporter a year or so ago."

The memories rushed over her as if it were yesterday. Her first time applying at the paper where her mother had worked had been when she was straight out of college, five years ago. They'd gone with a man then. A year ago, she'd read where they had an opening for an investigative reporter and had applied. The editor had told her they ended up promoting from within their own staff. She'd seen the man who'd stolen her position when she'd gone back to follow up on another position.

Jackson Devereaux.

How could she have ever forgotten his name? And those eyes? The same ones that pierced her now.

"Alyssa?"

The ghost of her mother mocked her, causing every nerve in her body to zing. "I don't know what you expect from me, Mr. Devereaux." She shoved to her feet on shaky legs, scraping the chair against the chipped tile floor. "I can't help you." She took a step backward. "I won't."

Her feet couldn't move fast enough as she ran out of the sandwich shop and across the street to the hospital. He called her name, but she refused to look back. Tears already blurred her vision, and she wouldn't give him the satisfaction of crying in front of him. Again. He might not have recognized her as the girl who'd broken down in tears at the death of her dream last year, but her heartache would all come out if she had to speak to him again.

She didn't stop her mad dash until she'd reached Grandmere's door. Alyssa paused in the hall, fighting to get her anguish and breathing under control. Why hadn't she recognized him immediately? She'd vowed that day to prove herself a better reporter than the lackey they'd promoted. Hadn't she committed his face to memory?

The door to Grandmere's room whooshed open, and CoCo skidded to a stop. "Al? What are you doing standing out here?" She laid a hand on Alyssa's arm. "Why, you're pale as a magnolia in full bloom. What's wrong?"

She couldn't confide in her sister about the mortification she'd endured. CoCo had never understood how much Alyssa had wanted that job—how she'd craved success so badly she could taste it rinsing out the tang of the bayou in her mouth. The job symbolic of her mother's legacy at the paper. When she'd been turned down, she suffered her worst humiliation. Even more so than the kids in school who'd taunted and tormented her because of her grandmother's position in the voodoo community.

"N-Nothing. I just got a little winded, I guess."

"The elevator still bother you?" CoCo's face filled with sympathy.

The last thing Alyssa wanted. CoCo couldn't realize Alyssa didn't have claustrophobia. No, Alyssa's fear derived from the small elevator car's similarity to a compact automobile. Being in the confined space made her hear the crunching metal, smell the smoke and fire.

"I'm fine." She fumbled for the lip balm to soothe her personal reminder of the crash. "How's Grandmere?"

"Eating lunch. I was about to run to the cafeteria and grab a bite. Want to come with me?"

Food was the last thing she wanted, but she didn't need CoCo getting suspicious. That would only lead to more questions—ones Alyssa refused to entertain. "I'm not really hungry, but I could use a cold drink."

Her sister broke out into a smile that lit up her tanned face, laced her hand through Alyssa's arm and led her down the hall. "We have so much to catch up on. How'd it go at the police station this morning?"

"They called in the FBI. They don't want me to leave until the case is wrapped up." Alyssa said the words without emotion, but her heart hammered. She certainly wasn't going to tell her sister about the strange sensations of being watched she'd been experiencing.

"You'll get to stay longer?"

"I suppose. I hope it's not an imposition."

"Don't be silly. This is your home, too." CoCo opened the door to the cafeteria.

No, the bayou wasn't—it never had been. She gritted her teeth. CoCo didn't seem to notice her angst, and charged ahead to the food line.

Alyssa had no choice but to follow.

Women were nothing if not confounding.

Jackson stared at his notes for the umpteenth time. What had he missed? He and Bubba had written out details of everything pertaining to the found money and the ensuing investigation. There had to be something here.

He leaned forward, resting his elbows on his knees, and

chewed on the pencil as he lifted his gaze. Outside, the wind kicked up a notch, tossing leaves in the air. Bubba's house seemed too quiet with him in the hospital. The silence distracted him. Speaking of distractions…Jackson couldn't get Alyssa LeBlanc out of his mind.

Replaying the scenario in the sandwich shop didn't give him any answers. She'd appeared interested, excited. Then something had changed. Her eyes had hardened, and she'd run out on him. He couldn't remember a time when a lady had actually fled from his attentions. Not that he'd revealed his interest to Alyssa. At least, he didn't think his attraction had been obvious.

What had he said to cause her to do such an about-face? He'd confessed to being a reporter, but that shouldn't have made a difference. They were in the same profession—she should understand his honesty in digging out the truth.

Jackson dropped the pencil to the coffee table. He stood and ran a hand over his hair. Had he ever written an unflattering story about her, or someone she cared about? Most of his articles weren't shining endorsements of the subject matter. He had a reputation for exposing people and scams, which had been the main reason Bubba'd called him to Lagniappe.

Buzzzzz!

His pocket vibrated. Jackson jerked out the Black-Berry. Ah, he had a message from his friend in the FBI.

SOUNDS LIKE YOU HAVE SOMETHING INTERESTING GOING ON IN PODUNK, U.S.A. OUR FIELD OFFICE SENT TWO AGENTS THERE TO INVESTIGATE ASSAULT ON A POLICE OFFICER. DO THESE RELATE? CARE TO SHARE?

NO BLUE PONTIACS HAVE BEEN REPORTED STOLEN
IN VERMILION PARISH IN THE LAST MONTH.
ALYSSA LEBLANC. LOTS OF BACKGROUND. SEND
FAX NUMBER AND I'LL SEND DETAILS.
WHAT ARE YOU MIXED UP IN THERE?

Jackson reread the message. So the car wasn't stolen. At least, not in this parish. Did the attackers use one of their own vehicles? Of course, they could've stolen the car from another parish. He'd have to check on that.

He stared at the last part of the message. The journalist in his gut urged him to send the fax number and get the details. Maybe the information could shed some light on Alyssa's bizarre behavior. But the Holy Spirit convinced him that sending the fax number wasn't the Christian thing to do. Getting information in this manner would be prying into someone's personal life. Yet, wasn't that what he did for a living—dig into people's private lives until he exposed the truth?

Had God called him to be a reporter, or had revealing people's darkest secrets always been in his nature? All this time, had he responded to the sins of the flesh, rather than walking in obedience to what his Lord and Savior had asked of him? Jackson dropped to his knees in the middle of Bubba's living room and lowered his head.

"Father God, I ask for wisdom in what You've called me to do. I'm not sure if I'm just nosy by nature. Have I been putting on airs and acting self-righteous when I have no right to?" His voice cracked as emotion clogged his throat. "Lord, I pray that right now, right this second, You cleanse my heart of any iniquities and impure motives. Let my life honor You. In Jesus's precious name, Amen."

He had no idea how long he sat on the worn carpet, but he refused to move from his prone position until peace enveloped him. When serenity finally came, he felt the answer he sought. He typed a reply to his friend's e-mail.

THANKS FOR THE INFO. MIGHT NEED YOU TO SPEAK UP FOR ME WITH THOSE TWO AGENTS. DESTROY THE INFO ON ALYSSA LEBLANC. DETAILS NOT NEEDED.

He jammed the BlackBerry into his back pocket and headed to the door. Time to go to work. He should get his chance to get into the office tonight. Getting closer to the truth fed his excitement as he drove to the port.

Night enveloped the docks. Water spray layered the wooden and concrete ports in slick mist. The crew of thirteen men loaded flats into cargos. Their off-color jokes and rowdy laughter crowded the air. Frank Thibodeaux, the man Bubba had set him up with to help him get temporary work, motioned him toward the office. Apparently, he'd passed Burl's "tryout" and would be put on payroll.

He slumped in the chair as he filled out the forms. His social security number would expose him. Jackson passed the forms across the desk to Frank. If he calculated correctly, the filing of his social security for taxes would come back within two weeks, and the jig would be up. He'd have to get the information he needed before then.

Frank slipped all the forms into a plain folder. "We'll leave it here for Brenda to enter when she comes in the morning." He stood and pulled on work gloves. "We'd better head on out before Burl wonders what's keeping us."

Jackson moved toward the hall. "Gotta use the facilities first."

Frank tossed him a concerned look, one that said he knew what Jackson was going to do, and opened the office door. "Hurry it up. I'll let Burl know we got you all squared away."

Once the man had trekked down the gangplank, Jackson yanked open the middle drawer of the metal filing cabinet. While he'd filled out his paperwork, he'd read the drawers' notations. The middle drawer held all the bills of lading.

He flipped through the folders, silently thanking the woman he'd never seen who did the office work. She filed the bills in numerical order. He pulled the three numbers matching the bags of money, and slipped them into the copy machine. Jackson glanced out the window. No one approached the gangplank. He let out a short sigh of relief.

Grabbing the copies and shoving them into his jacket pocket, Jackson quickly refiled the bills and closed the drawer. Movement out the window caught his attention.

Burl.

Coming up the gangplank.

Jackson glanced down. The copies couldn't be hidden well enough in his jacket to stand up to his boss's scrutiny.

He shoved the copies under the edge of a drawer and ran to the bathroom, barely having time to shut the door before he heard the squeak of the office's entrance opening. He flushed the toilet, turned on the faucet and ran his hands under the cold water.

"You sick?" Burl asked when Jackson stepped into the hall.

"I'm fine."

Burl grunted. "Then get to work. Lots of shipments coming in tonight."

"Yes, sir." He'd have to wait until later to retrieve the copied bills of lading.

SIX

Could life, for once, be so easy?

The morning sun teased around the edges of the kitchen curtains. Alyssa shook her head and dialed the number listed in the white pages. In Shreveport, politicians didn't have listed home numbers. Apparently in Lagniappe, they did. How convenient.

"Mouton residence."

They had someone to answer calls on a Saturday, too. Very cool. "This is Alyssa LeBlanc. I'd like to speak to Mr. Mouton regarding my mother, Claire LeBlanc."

"Please hold."

Who had music on their home hold option? The Moutons, that's who. Alyssa ran a finger over the scar under her lip, hoping the use of her mother's name would at least get her a response. The kitchen counter dug into her hip.

"Ms. LeBlanc? This is Edmond Mouton. How can I help you?"

Her stomach knotted. Oh, yeah, she'd gotten a response all right. From the senator himself. Alyssa gripped the phone tighter. "Senator Mouton, my mother was a photojournalist, Claire Le—"

"Yes, yes. I remember Claire very well. Lovely woman. Tragedy what happened to her. A crying shame. What can I do for you?"

Every single line she'd mentally prepared flew out of her mind. "Er, well, I'm, uh…" Oh, she needed to snap out of this. She straightened her shoulders. "I'm a reporter with the *Shreveport Times,* and I wondered if you'd grant me an interview." There, she'd said it.

"And you thought using your mother's name would encourage me to comply with your request?"

Busted. What could she say? "Well, yes."

His laugh came as suddenly as his words. "Very good, young lady. Your mother had the same kind of spunk. I like that. How about Monday at ten, here at my house?"

Alyssa scrambled to write down the address on a scrap of paper. "Thank you, Senator Mouton."

"Don't disappoint me by being late."

She replaced the phone, adrenaline zipping through her veins. She had a scoop! That would prove her better than Jackson Devereaux and his single dimple. She danced a jig in the middle of the sunny kitchen, barefoot and all.

"What's got you in such a happy mood?"

Alyssa spun and faced her younger sister. "Tara!" In two steps, she pulled the young woman into her arms and gave a stiff hug.

Tara laughed, stepping out of the embrace. "What's up with you, Al?"

"I just got an exclusive interview."

"Good for you." Tara moved to the icebox and grabbed a soft drink.

Alyssa took notice of her sister's outfit—a pair of ratty jeans and a T-shirt that had seen one too many washings. She would have thought Tara was in for the night, except that she wore a pair of scuffed sneakers, a telltale sign she planned on going out, since Tara never wore shoes if she could avoid them. "Where are you going?

"Out."

"Dressed like that?" The words jumped out of her mouth before she could insert any tact.

A disgusted smirk crossed Tara's pretty face. She set her can on the counter with a resounding thud. "Yeah, dressed like this."

"Is that really proper attire for a bookkeeper?" Why couldn't she just shut up? Tara worked in a jazz club after closing, for pity's sake.

"For me it is. Got a problem with my clothes?"

Just. Don't. Say. Anything. "Uh, no." Alyssa ran a hand over her own jeans, with creases still neatly down the front. "Maybe we can do something together and catch up."

"Al, don't tell me you're going to get all mushy like CoCo. Don't go there."

"I just want to visit with you for a little while." Did her voice sound as whiny as she thought?

"Before you hoof it back up north, ya mean?" Tara flipped her long straight hair over her shoulder and narrowed her eyes. The rivalry between north and south Louisiana glared in her eyes. "You don't care about what's going on here in Lagniappe. You never did."

She couldn't argue that point even if she wanted to— her tongue felt four sizes too big for her mouth. Alyssa swallowed and cleared her throat. "It's not that I don't care about y'all—" there she went again, resorting to the slang she detested "—I just don't care for this back-woods town."

"You proved that by running away as soon as you

could." Tara's eyes, so similar to Alyssa's own, were nothing more than slits in her smooth, tanned face.

"That's not fair. I had to get out, do something, make something of myself."

"Because you always thought you were too good for Lagniappe."

"We're all too good for this hick town. Can't you see that?" Alyssa's voice went up an octave.

"No, this is my home, Al. It's a pity you never understood that."

"It's not home. We were all born and raised in New Orleans, Tara. Even you, although you like to pretend you were born in this forsaken bayou. Playing around with Grandmere's voodoo and such." Alyssa shook her head. "Momee would be ashamed of you and CoCo. She wanted more for us, all of us. She set out to make something of herself. Something big. Why do you think she never moved here after she and Papa married?"

"For someone who belongs to an organization that thrives on heritage, you sure want to bury yours."

Ouch. That hurt. "The United Daughters of the Confederacy are committed to preserving the heritage of our ancestors who fought for the Confederacy, and—"

Tara held up her hand. "Stop. I've heard your spiel already. You'd think with what CoCo uncovered about Grandpere's heritage, you'd steer clear of all that."

Of course, the revelation a couple of months ago about her grandfather's involvement in the Ku Klux Klan *had* been a cause of embarrassment to her, but she didn't want to share that with Tara now. "Just because Grandpere belonged to the Klan doesn't mean we should ignore the men who stood up for—"

"You go play in your white dresses, hats and gloves, and I'll deal with the spirits. Let's just leave it at that."

Alyssa opened her mouth to argue, but Tara had already spun around and stormed from the kitchen. The screen door slamming indicated she'd left.

That went well. Alyssa had wanted to reach out to her younger sister, show her that she'd waste away in this horrid place. And the influence of Grandmere's voodoo ways were corrupting her little sister's mind, just as it had CoCo's. Fortunately, CoCo had come to her senses a few years ago and stopped dabbling in such nonsense. But not Tara. She'd taken up experimenting full force.

Alyssa sighed. She'd managed to anger Tara, further alienating herself. Why did this family thing have to be so hard? Was she some kind of reject, not even able to bond with her sisters, her own flesh and blood?

She threw Tara's soda can into the trash and passed a towel over the already clean counter. A glance at the clock told her CoCo would be back from her morning bayou run soon. Should she start something for breakfast? Alyssa hadn't ever been the cook in the family. CoCo, now that girl could cook. Tara wasn't so bad, either, but Alyssa was a misfit in the kitchen.

Bam! Bam! Bam!

Alyssa started, then marched into the hallway where she could see the front door. Tara had only closed the screen, leaving her a view of the veranda and its occupant.

Jackson Devereaux stood in the frame, filling the space. Did he have to look so devastatingly handsome this early in the morning?

He smiled as he spied her. "Hi. Can I talk to you for a minute?"

Rats. Too late to pretend she hadn't heard him. She crossed her arms over her chest. "I don't have anything to say to you."

"Please, Alyssa. I don't know what I did to set you off."

How about taking my job, for a start? The one that would've honored her mother's memory.

"Will you at least talk to me?"

She let out a long sigh. He wouldn't go away until she spoke to him. Fine. She'd hear him out and then send him on his way. Alyssa pushed open the door. He barely managed to step back before the door hit him.

She stepped onto the porch and sat in one of the oversize rocking chairs on the veranda. "Fine. What do you want to talk about?"

He lowered his tall form into the rocker beside her. "Why'd you run out of the deli on me?"

Because on principle, I can't stand you. "I just didn't want to talk anymore." She fought the urge to fidget by clasping her hands together demurely in her lap. "It was useless to discuss anything further."

"You know I didn't feed you a line. I could tell your reporter instincts kicked in. You know this is a prime story just waiting to be written."

She dropped her gaze to the wooden planks of the veranda. Anything to avoid meeting his stare. "It doesn't matter what I think." *I'm only a reporter at a small paper. Not like your big one.*

"It does to me." His voice floated like a whisper on the bayou breeze.

How could his voice cause such a reaction in her gut? He had to be playing her. She needed to remember he was the enemy, for all practical purposes.

Alyssa lifted her chin and studied his eyes. She couldn't detect any deception lurking there. Her mouth suddenly felt as dry as the Spanish moss hanging on the cypress trees. "Why?"

"I don't know." He leaned back and smiled. That single dimple added character to his rugged face. "I just care."

"I see." Her pulse spiked. She hadn't a clue why, aside from the fact that Jackson was good-looking, in an out-doorsy sort of way that normally didn't appeal to her. But on him...well, she had to admit, his eyes got her every time. Worse than a puppy dog's.

Oh, man, she'd started thinking of him by his first name again. That could be trouble. She needed to snap out of it. This man had stolen her job—the one that would've made her mother proud.

"I know this could be a big story, for both of us. We aren't really in competition. We could both have articles running in our papers simultaneously. Couldn't we work together to find out who attacked Bubba? I'm positive the assault is linked to the money drop case."

If she worked with him, she could drag out the story, sending Simon small teaser articles to get readership. Of course, she'd also do the piece on Senator Mouton. By the time the Feds wrapped up the case, she could have two or three lead stories. All with her byline. That'd teach little Ms. Marlee who got the ace reporter tagline.

And what about Simon's favorite line? Keep your friends close, but your enemies closer. If she played her cards right, maybe, just maybe, she could scoop Jackson and prove to his stuffy old editor he'd made the wrong choice years ago. Maybe he'd give her a second chance.

"At least it'd give you something to do in this Podunk

town. Since you're stuck here and all, *chère*." He smiled, the dimple making her heart do funny somersaults.

"Okay. Since I'm stuck here, as you so eloquently put it." *And I want to steal your job.*

His grin widened, her heartbeat quickened. She really needed to get a grip on herself. Handsome men were a dime a dozen. Well, maybe not, but she needed to focus. Not let her emotions cause her to make hasty decisions.

"Where do we start?" Alyssa pushed to her feet, steeling her adolescent, crush-like feelings.

She refused to become attracted to the man she'd use to climb her way to the top.

What went on inside that complicated head of hers? Alyssa LeBlanc had flipped sides on him again, as quickly and efficiently as she had at lunch. She puzzled his mind, and his sentiments. Maybe that's why he'd sought out a local to direct him to the LeBlanc plantation home and driven over before he could talk himself out of it.

The bewitching woman now peered at him from beneath dark lashes. He'd always been a sucker for killer eyes, and Alyssa's amazed him.

"Do you have any leads?"

He snapped himself out of his silent assessment of her intriguing traits. "I have some notes at Bubba's place. I've gone over them, but there's something I'm missing."

"Need a fresh pair of eyes, huh?"

"Yeah. So, you wanna follow me back to Bubba's?"

"I don't think so. Alone in a house with a man I really don't know? Are you kidding?"

He should've known better. This wasn't New Orleans. People talked in little towns. "How about we go out to eat? Someplace quiet where you can look over what I've gotten so far."

The hum of an airboat filled the air.

She flashed a slight smile. "I have a better idea. Do you know the location of the money drops the sheriff found?"

He gave a little shrug. "I have a marker number he wrote down. Committed it to memory. Whatever it means."

She smiled as a woman banked an airboat, jumped to the ground and headed to the stairs near them. "Perfect."

The woman stood about an inch taller than Alyssa, with long curly dark hair. She held out her hand. "CoCo LeBlanc, Alyssa's sister."

"This is Jackson Devereaux." Alyssa touched her sister's shoulder. "I wonder if you could take me and Mr. Devereaux out to a specific marker in the bayou."

Slick. Smart thinking, too. He watched the interplay of emotions cross CoCo's face as she studied her sister.

"You want me to take you out in my airboat? Into the bayou? Now?"

"Please." Alyssa and CoCo seemed to be carrying on a conversation with their eyes. Downright eerie.

Finally, CoCo quirked a single eyebrow. "Okay. Give me a second to run inside."

He watched her enter the house before turning to Alyssa. "Will she know where the markers are?"

"Oh, CoCo knows this bayou better than anybody."

"Really?" He couldn't imagine that speck of a woman knowing the swamp better than some of the gator hunters or fishermen. "What's she do?"

Alyssa's eyes twinkled in the setting sun. "She's an alligator conservationist."

SEVEN

The hum of the large fan behind the seats was deafening as the airboat skimmed over the bayou. Water sprayed up, misting them all. Jackson stared at CoCo admiringly. Alyssa couldn't believe it. A cultured man impressed by a woman steering an airboat on a bayou? No, he couldn't be. But a funny feeling threatened to suffocate Alyssa, a strange sensation that made Alyssa see her sister in a new light. One that cast very attractive shadows around CoCo.

"How's Luc?" she blurted out. Man, she hoped her tone didn't sound as desperate as she felt.

CoCo shot her a hard stare before diverting her attention back to the waterline. "He's fine. Wants to come over for supper tomorrow night and see you. Especially if Grandmere comes home."

Alyssa nodded at Jackson. "Luc's her boyfriend."

"I see."

"What's the marker number again?" CoCo asked.

He rattled off the number. CoCo slowed the boat and slowly turned the wheel. "Should be up here on your right." Her gaze scanned the waterline. "There." She pointed to a nook around a bend.

The area formed a cove. An island, no bigger than twelve

feet by twelve feet, held nothing but cypress trees and lichen, all bent and covering the small recess like a canopy.

A perfect place for a money drop. Out of the way. Blocked by aerial view unless you knew where to look.

CoCo turned off the big fan powering the airboat and nudged the control of the trolling motor. The boat hummed toward the nook's slight opening. "Why'd you want to see this marker point?"

"An article I'm working on," Jackson said smoothly as his gaze took in all the details of the area.

"You're a reporter? Like Alyssa?"

"Yeah. Can you get me closer? I want to get on that island."

"I can get you closer, but there's probably not much solid ground. More like quicksand and murk." But CoCo steered the airboat to the biggest clump of trees.

Alyssa leaned toward Jackson. "What do you think?"

"I think it's ideal for a drop site," he whispered.

The boat drifted until the nose tapped cypress roots. An eerie silence shrouded the bayou. Miniature palmettos rippled in the gentle breeze. The swamp seemed to be holding its breath in expectancy. Of what, Alyssa had no idea, but goosebumps pimpled her arms.

"What, exactly, are you looking for?" CoCo asked.

Jackson shrugged. "Just anything out of place."

"Hmm." CoCo stared into the clump of trees. "There. See that bit of cloth near the waterline? That doesn't belong." She glanced at her notebook clipped alongside the steering controls. "It wasn't here last week when I did my inventory."

Energy thrummed through Alyssa. "Can you get us there?"

"I can try." CoCo engaged the trolling motor, slowly moving the boat.

Seconds dragged on like minutes as the craft inched its way over the murky waters. CoCo settled the airboat against soil. "That's as close as we can get."

Jackson stood, already pulling a digital camera from his shirt pocket. "Let me see if I can get it."

"Be careful," CoCo warned.

He set one foot on the ground, then the other. "Feels okay."

Alyssa rubbed the scar under her lip as she watched every movement he made. "Is there a way to get here without a boat?"

"See that point there?" CoCo gestured to a craggy outreaching part of land, almost touching the island. "That's right off Milo Point Road. The swamp isn't deep over there, so you could probably wade from the point to the island."

Alyssa gauged the distance between the point and the island to be about fifty feet. She wouldn't wade in the icky water that far, but a drug dealer who wanted his money probably would. She turned her gaze back to Jackson.

His steps were slow but sure as he crept toward the cloth in the marshy pit. He stopped a few feet out and snapped several pictures from different angles. Seemingly satisfied, he grabbed the cloth and faced the boat. He held the cloth over his head. "Success!"

A loud rumbling nearly knocked Alyssa from the edge of her seat. Her heart hammered louder than the airboat's fan.

CoCo jumped to her feet. "Jackson, don't move." She

retrieved a small noisemaker gadget. Pressing the button, a higher-pitched roar filled the air.

"What?" Jackson asked.

"Just don't move." CoCo sounded the horrible growl again. She put the noisemaker closer to the water and pressed the button once more.

"What are you doing?" Alyssa couldn't see what had her sister in such a panic, but she knew by the serious look on CoCo's face that something wasn't right.

"Moodoo's in the area. That's his growl."

Alyssa glanced around. She didn't see anybody. "Who, pray tell, is Moodoo?"

"One of my gators." CoCo sounded the horrific noise again.

Shivers tickled Alyssa's spine. An alligator? One of her sister's? Jackson stood in the line of danger! She met his frightened stare.

He hadn't moved, but his gaze darted around the area. "What is it?"

A large bulk moved toward the boat at a surprisingly fast rate. The alligator hit the water so smoothly, a splash didn't even mar the level line of the water. Only a gentle ripple. A bump hit against the boat.

CoCo chuckled. "Hey, boy. Took you long enough." She reached into a bag and tossed something out into the open water. The big reptile sped toward it. CoCo turned back to Jackson. "Hurry up and get back in the boat, for goodness sake."

Jackson's face had paled. His stare locked onto the alligator, following the beast's movements with his eyes, and his feet appeared to have taken root.

"Jackson!" Alyssa's heart thrummed.

He darted his gaze to meet hers.

"Come on. Hurry."

The urgency in her voice must have snapped him out of his fear-induced trance. He quickly boarded the boat and dropped to the seat. "That was interesting."

CoCo threw something else out into the water and put the trolling motor in reverse. "It's odd. Moodoo isn't normally in this part of the bayou. Something had to have snagged his attention."

"Like what?" Alyssa couldn't believe she could sit calmly and discuss an alligator's behavior.

"An airboat like mine. He thinks they're all me, which is why some poachers were able to hurt him about a year ago. I nursed him back to health, but he didn't learn his lesson." Her forehead wrinkled. "But the boat would've had to have been here for at least a day for the vibrations to have beckoned him. And I haven't been near this part of the bayou in a week."

"You have a pet alligator?" Alyssa couldn't fathom her sister's strange interests.

CoCo chuckled as she fired up the big fan powering the boat. "Not exactly. Animals just remember sounds and actions. Gators, in particular, are very smart."

"If you say so." Alyssa sniffed.

"What else could've drawn him into this area?" Jackson still clutched the cloth in a death grip.

"Hmm." CoCo spun the boat into open water and sped over the bayou. "Something he hunted could've led him there. Although once he caught his prey, he would've gone back to familiar waters."

Jackson remained quiet, as if mulling over the information.

"Anything else?" The reporter in Alyssa refused to be silenced by her distaste.

"Activity in the area would draw him and make him stick around. But there's not much movement in that part of the bayou. As you saw, it's pretty secluded and not many people would be brave enough to venture so far in."

Which would make the location a perfect place to drop drug money.

"So, if there was activity going on here, it'd have to be someone who knew the bayou pretty well, right?" Jackson asked.

"*Oui.* But few people know that part very well." CoCo slowed the boat as they neared the LeBlanc landing.

"Who would?" Alyssa refused to be outquestioned by the big shot New Orleans reporter.

CoCo killed the engine and grabbed a rope. "I don't know. Me, the Wildlife and Fisheries group, some environmentalists. Not too many people." She tied off the boat and jumped to the ground.

Alyssa and Jackson stood and moved to follow.

CoCo held up her hand. "Now, who wants to fill me in on what's going on?"

How could two sisters be so different?

Jackson shook his head at how blasé Alyssa was with her older sister. She'd been evasive, giving just enough facts to satisfy CoCo's curiosity. Surprisingly, CoCo had let the matter drop with her sister's half excuse, rushing into the house to start lunch and leaving him alone with Alyssa out by his truck.

"Let me see it," Alyssa demanded once her sister had shut the screen door.

He didn't have to ask what she wanted. The cloth. He'd shoved it into his pocket as soon as he'd gotten situated on the boat. Now he pulled the cloth free from the denim.

The plain cotton fabric, which had originally been pastel blue, was now dingy gray. A set of numbers splayed across the strip, written with a black marker—0211.

"What's that mean?" Alyssa peered into his face, her eyes wider than normal, allowing him to see the little green flecks around the edges. Fascinating.

"I don't know. A tracking number, maybe? Could be a date or time."

"Where do we go from here?" She shifted her weight, slight as she appeared, from one foot to the other.

"Why don't I grab my notes and see if there's anything remotely similar?"

"Not without me, you don't."

Afraid he'd leave her out of the scoop. He didn't bother to hide his smile. "I had no intention of that. Earlier, I offered you a meal while you looked over the notes."

"Oh." She rubbed her finger over that little circle under her lip. "That sounds good."

"Would you like to follow me in your car, or can you trust yourself in the same vehicle with me?"

Fire lit her eyes. "Trust myself? Please. Don't flatter yourself, Mr. Devereaux."

Jackson chuckled. "Then shall we?" He made a sweeping gesture toward the passenger side of the truck.

"Let me tell CoCo I'm leaving."

She disappeared into the house and returned quickly. Alyssa threw him a final glare before stomping to the passenger side and yanking the handle before he could. She scooted into the seat and reached to close the door, but he held it. Her eyes flashed.

"Where I'm from, it's considered polite to open doors for a lady, *chère*."

She snorted before he shut her inside.

Oh, yeah, Alyssa LeBlanc was one fascinating woman.

He slipped behind the steering wheel and turned toward Bubba's house on the other side of the bayou. The sun danced overhead, tossing hot rays through the truck's windshield.

"Tell me about your friendship with the sheriff."

"We went to college together. Old frat buddies."

"Keep in touch?"

"Pretty much. E-mail's made it easy. Bubba's not too big on that, though. He prefers the phone."

"I see."

Did she? Probably not. She had no way of knowing Bubba'd been the one who pulled him out of his downward spiral of drinking and drug use. No one knew Bubba had saved him, in more ways than one. He'd been the one to introduce Jackson to Christ. Months after Jackson had dried out, he'd made the decision to dedicate his life to Jesus. He hadn't looked back on his old lifestyle since.

"Where's a good place to eat where we can have some privacy?"

"I don't know. I don't live here." Her tone grated against his sensibilities.

"But you used to. For several years."

"It's changed. I've changed. The only places I went when I lived here were high school hangouts."

Something aside from snappiness crept into her tone. Almost…pain. He took his gaze off the road. She'd turned her head to stare out the window. O-kay. Topic off-limits. He'd let that go. For now. "Bubba told me the Crawfish Café has pretty good grub."

"All right." She still wouldn't look at him.

He pulled into Bubba's driveway. "Won't take me but a minute to grab my notes." He left the truck running while he darted inside.

He grabbed the notebook and file, his heart pounding. But his erratic heartbeat had nothing to do with the heat or the fast pace with which he headed back to the truck— it had everything to do with the woman waiting for him.

EIGHT

The perky young waitress stopped at their table, pen poised over her notepad. "Have y'all decided what you want?" She popped her gum as often as Missy, the police dispatcher.

"I'll have the boiled crawfish platter and iced tea."

Alyssa glanced at the waitress. "The same, please."

The teenybopper in a standard waitress apron swiped the menus and bounded toward the kitchen.

Jackson passed her a plain manila folder once the waitress had disappeared behind the swinging door. "This is a copy of the police file Bubba gave me. I made notes from conversations with him and my own observations."

She glanced at the notes written in neat scrawl, her mind reeling. "Okay, the sheriff found the first bag of money three weeks ago where CoCo took us in the bayou."

"Right."

She ran her finger down the page. "He found another one last week at the same place."

"When he called me."

Turning the page, she detected a different handwriting. She raised her gaze to Jackson and quirked a brow.

"Those are Bubba's notes detailing his investigation for two weeks."

"Ah." She scanned the information quicker than her mind could process the data. One line stuck out at her. "Says here he found one of those pieces of cloth tied to the money bag. Both times." She squinted to make out the rough handwriting. "0418 and 1121."

"What do you make of that?"

"Says he checked and the number wasn't a boat identifier." Her eyes widened. "He contacted DEA, and they told him unless he found proof of drugs, they couldn't help him?"

"That's our government dollars at work, *chère*."

"It's outrageous." Disappointment hung in her voice and heart more than shock.

"Does it surprise you?"

"Unfortunately, no. He asked two of his deputies to assist in the investigation. He officially opened a case and logged the money into evidence."

Jackson started to speak, but the waitress chose that moment to deliver their plates. He waited until she'd left and he'd said grace before he nodded at the folder. "We didn't get to discuss which two deputies."

"He never said?" She pushed the file to the side and lifted a mudbug.

"I didn't think it important to ask. Now I'm wondering if one of those men was somehow involved in his attack."

"Maybe their names are on the case record?"

"Like I can see it now that the FBI thinks I'm an official suspect?"

She snapped off the head of a crawfish and sucked. Cayenne pepper and Tony Chachere's Seasoning tingled her taste buds. Even though Shreveport was in the same state, nobody cooked spicy food like deep South Louisianans.

"So, why leave the cloths?"

"Maybe the person retrieving got rushed? Or maybe it was dark outside and they didn't realize it'd fallen off."

"Could be, but that doesn't make a whole lot of sense."

"Nothing about this is exactly logical." She took a sip of her drink. "I just don't see how it's all linked."

"Okay, here's my stab at the scenario." Jackson wiped his hands on his napkin, then laced his fingers over his plate. "It's drug smuggling. Bubba finds the money, opens a file. He assigns two deputies to the case. He follows standard procedure on the investigation."

"Sounds right. Keep going."

"But one or both of the deputies are dirty. Or maybe involved in the drug deals in some offhand way. He tells the smugglers what Bubba found."

Her mind pounded with the possibilities. "So they decided to take the sheriff out." She shook her head. "But why leave him alive?"

"To teach him a lesson? Besides, killing an officer would attract even more attention."

"This is getting complicated." Yet, the situation had all the earmarks of a big story—drugs, police corruption, attempted murder. Simon was wrong; the entire state would be interested in this story.

"You know, maybe you could try and find out something more."

She dropped the carcass of a crawfish to her plate. "From whom?"

"The deputies? That Gary Anderson seemed interested in you."

Snorting, she wiped her fingers, now coated bright red, on the wet towelette. "Yeah. Right."

"One of those Fed boys looked attractive enough to think all women doted on him."

"You mean the guy from the Federal Bureau of Intimidation?"

Jackson laughed, nearly sputtering the iced tea he'd just sipped. "Haven't heard that one before."

She smiled, choosing to ignore his asinine suggestion. "What do you think these numbers mean?"

"Could be a code to indicate what the payment's for. Or a date or time."

"Sounds plausible." Alyssa wiped her mouth, pushing away her plate. "How do we break it?"

"We just keep digging."

She liked the way he thought. Slick. "What're we waiting for?"

Rain had lessened the humidity, but moisture was still heavy in the air. Even the inside of Bubba's house felt damp. Sticky.

"I made copies of the bills of lading at the dock, but I can't retrieve them until Monday night when I go back to work."

She pressed her lips together in a fine line, making that little pink circle more prominent against her pale face. He had the sudden urge to touch it. He clenched his fists in response. "Alyssa, if you want to stop investigating with me, I'll understand. This reeks of danger. Bubba's barely hanging on."

"No. I want to know what's happening." She shivered and hugged herself. "I'm already in danger."

He took a step closer to her, the instinct to protect so strong. "How's that?"

"If a cop is involved, then they know I heard someone's voice the night they dumped the sheriff."

Chills crept up his spine. How could he have missed the connection? He gave in to instinct and wrapped an arm around her shoulders.

Did she have to be so logical? He didn't like the idea of her being in danger. He'd seen what they did to Bubba.

She ran her fingers through her spiky bangs and shook her head. "No, I have to follow through on this."

"I understand, but we need to be careful." He stared at her, picturing Bubba's injuries on her.

"Very careful."

NINE

Spinning out of control. Hot, so hot. Metal grinding.
  Screaming—was it hers?
  So hot.
  Pain on her face, under her lip.
  Crying.
  So hot. So painful.

Alyssa bolted out of bed, ignoring the tears wetting her cheeks, and headed to the window. Stupid nightmares. Worse now that she was here in Lagniappe. In Shreveport, she could ignore the nightmares, memories and the past. But not here. Never in Lagniappe. She sucked in air, forcing her breathing to steady.

Bright streaks of yellow and orange zigzagged through the cloudless sky as the sun ushered in Sunday morning. She watched CoCo bank and tie off the airboat. The past couple of times she'd been back in Lagniappe, Alyssa had noticed a subtle change in her older sister. Not so emotional, calmer, more at peace with life in general. Maybe CoCo's relationship with Luc made the difference. Well, not quite. This was the first time Alyssa had returned to Lagniappe since the two had gotten back together. What had brought about the transformation in her sister? Maturity, perhaps? Nah. CoCo was only two years older than Alyssa's twenty-seven.

The front screen door slammed, jarring Alyssa from her musings. She'd been so deep in thought she hadn't even noticed her sister leaving the boat. Alyssa took a final glance at the morning. The sun had crested over the tree line, throwing a warm glow into the sky. If she were anywhere but the bayou, she would've been impressed by the beauty and grace of nature. She'd always begun her day by checking out the window. Funny how she'd forgotten her ritual.

"Al? You up?" CoCo hollered from the bottom of the stairs.

Tightening the sash of her robe, Alyssa moved to the landing at the top of the staircase. "Yes."

"I thought we could have breakfast together before church."

Church? Oh, yes, right. CoCo attended the community church sitting outside Lagniappe town limits. She'd invited Alyssa to attend the last time Alyssa had visited. She hadn't been able to then as she'd been anxious to head back to Shreveport. Today held no such timetable.

"Sure. Sounds like a plan."

"I'll put the biscuits in the oven before I hop in the shower. Coffee's ready whenever you are."

Alyssa dressed quickly, not sure what these hicks wore to worship services. After all, they'd never attended as girls. Why, the ceiling would fall if voodoo priestess Marie LeBlanc set foot inside a church. Alyssa chose a simple black skirt with a white silk blouse. After applying her makeup with a light hand, she checked her appearance in the mirror. Her hair had once been as long and wavy as CoCo's. As dark, too.

Determined to shed the spawn of a voodoo queen persona when she escaped the bayou, she'd embraced a drastic haircut and coloring job. Alyssa LeBlanc had re-created herself, inside and out. As she surveyed her reflection, a sense of pride filled her. She no longer resembled that mousy little girl, and she'd masterminded the conversion all by herself.

"Bacon's on," CoCo called out.

How did the woman shower and dress in the time Alyssa took to put on her makeup?

Alyssa entered the kitchen amid the mouth-watering smell of pepper bacon and chicory blend coffee. Her stomach rumbled in appreciation. CoCo stood at the stove dressed in a pair of khaki slacks and basic cotton T-shirt. Surely she wasn't wearing *that* to church services?

CoCo nodded as Alyssa poured a cup of coffee. "Sit down. It's all done."

Not only had her sister showered and dressed, she'd also cooked breakfast. Alyssa swallowed back her prickliness, taking note of her own feelings of inadequacy. That's what this was—that old sensation of never measuring up, plain and simple. The bayou brought out the worst in her. Always had.

CoCo offered up a quick prayer over the food, then pulled back the kitchen curtains. "Looks like it's going to be a glorious day." The smile made her eyes glow.

Alyssa didn't reply. She sliced open the buttermilk biscuit and slipped a pat of butter inside the flaky layers. The amazing mix melted in her mouth. How come she couldn't bake like this? Yet another screaming declaration of her inferiority. Now her nerves truly rankled.

She cast her gaze to her sister's attire again. "Are you wearing that to church?"

"*Oui.* Why?"

"Isn't it a bit, um, casual?" Alyssa bit a hunk off a slice of bacon to avoid adding any more censure to her tone. She chewed slowly, biding time.

"*Boo,* God doesn't care what I wear."

"But people do."

"Al, when are you going to get it that I don't answer to others? None of us do. We simply have to please God, and I'm pretty certain what I put on my body matters not to Him."

"When are you going to understand that appearances are important?"

"Not to me."

"It matters to me."

Those words bounced around in her mind, settling in her chest. Appearances did matter. People judged how you looked and presented yourself. Alyssa had fought too hard to elevate herself to an acceptable level. She wouldn't let anyone or anything knock her down.

CoCo let out a heavy sigh. "If it bothers you so much, I'll change into a skirt."

"Thank you." The last bite of biscuit stuck in her throat. Alyssa gulped down the rest of her coffee, thankfully now warm and not scalding. She shoved back her chair and lifted her plate. "I'll do the dishes while you change."

She finished the dishes before CoCo met her at the front door.

"Luc's meeting us there." CoCo grabbed her keys from the hook.

Great. Now she'd get to see the happy couple up close and personal. Just something else she'd managed to fail to do—have a decent love life. Who was she kidding? She didn't even have a love life, decent or otherwise. Dismay tugged against her heart.

"Tara called earlier," CoCo said as she headed to the Jeep. "Grandmere will be released early this afternoon."

Alyssa slipped into the passenger's seat. "Do you think she's well enough to come home so soon?"

"Her doctors think so." CoCo put the Jeep in gear and gunned the engine.

"I don't know. I think I'd feel better if we got a second opinion."

"I trust them." CoCo steered the Jeep down the dirt road. "Besides, Grandmere's chomping at the bit to get out."

"I bet. Probably wants to concoct some potion or something."

CoCo laughed. "More than likely."

"You know, we could clean out her shed before she gets home, and she wouldn't be able to do that voodoo business."

"That would only upset her, and she'd simply go out and get more herbs."

"Why haven't you put a stop to all this nonsense?"

"I'd like to, Al. I really would, but I can't just put my foot down. This is all Grandmere has ever known, and breaking her of it takes time. And finesse."

"It's a disgrace."

"It may be, but I'm praying the Holy Spirit will continue to work on Grandmere."

Alyssa swallowed a snort.

"You know you were asking me about that island in the bayou?" CoCo asked, then continued without a response. "That's Milo Point Road right there. You'd follow the pavement until it dead-ends, then walk out to the outlying point."

Interesting. She should go check that out.

CoCo whipped into the parking lot of a small white church. Paint peeled off the worn wood. The steeple leaned to the side just a tad. Lovely. Worshipping in a broken-down, skimpy church. No velvet-padded pews would await them. No state-of-the-art sound system would saturate the sanctuary with music. Alyssa pressed her lips together and followed her sister up the rickety wood steps.

A young man in jeans and a T-shirt extended his hand. "Good morning. I'm Pastor Spencer Bertrand, but everyone calls me Spence." He shook her hand with a firm grip. "Welcome."

This young man was the preacher? With his dark hair all shaggy, he looked more like a hippie than a pastor. Mercy, what could he know about preaching? "Uh, thank you."

At the second pew from the front, CoCo slipped in beside her boyfriend, who stood as they approached.

"Morning, Alyssa. Nice to see you again." Luc Trahan's smile danced in his eyes.

"You, too."

Luc's arm was draped behind her sister's shoulders. Alyssa studied them from the corner of her eye. They made a handsome couple. Luc, with his tall form and broad shoulders, not to mention his extraordinary good looks, complemented CoCo's small features. Next to him, CoCo looked delicate and fragile.

Why couldn't Alyssa find someone who accepted her for who she was like Luc did CoCo?

The first chords from the organ filled the church. The congregation rose to its feet and followed along in the hymnal.

Never had worship music sounded so beautiful. She closed her eyes, letting the words wash over her. How long had it been since she felt like this? Ever?

Alyssa studied CoCo's face. Eyes closed, her sister sang with a smile void of any worry or stress. The picture snagged Alyssa's heart.

Could *this* be the source of CoCo's peace?

Alyssa had captured his attention before she'd even entered the church, as if he had radar tuned in exclusively to her coordinates.

Jackson sat in the back pew, studying the clean lines of her back. He groaned silently. He hadn't come for this. He'd chosen to attend the small church on the outskirts of town to avoid seeing any of the Lagniappe locals. Yet, there sat the source of his discord, jarring his thoughts from communion with God.

Her presence here, did that confirm her a Christian? Jackson had known a lot of people in his life who'd attended church faithfully but had never given their hearts to Jesus Christ. He personally didn't get that.

The preacher took his place behind the pulpit and read a Scripture from the Book of Psalms. The forty-sixth, to be exact.

"God is our refuge and strength, an ever-present help in trouble. Therefore we will not fear. Though the earth give way and the mountains fall into the heart of the sea, though its waters roar and foam and the mountains quake with their surging."

The Scripture…as if the preacher spoke directly to Jackson's heart with God's word. No matter how uncertain things in this life—his attraction to Alyssa, the attack on Bubba, the case itself—one thing was sure: God would never leave him.

The praise and worship this small church had could compete with any Jackson had ever experienced. He'd definitely be back next week. Maybe they had a Wednesday night service, as well.

Situated in the back of the church, Jackson was one of the first to exit and shake Spencer Bertrand's hand. "Wonderful service."

The man who couldn't be much older than Jackson smiled and gripped his hand tighter. "Glad you enjoyed it."

Jackson intended to rush to his vehicle and get away before Alyssa could catch sight of him. He didn't need to avoid her, but he wanted to go home and read the Scripture in his own Bible before he went to check on Bubba. Let the words soak into his very soul.

"Good morning, Mr. Devereaux."

Too late. Alyssa's sister called out to him.

He turned and planted a smile. "Morning, Ms. LeBlanc."

CoCo and what had to be her boyfriend descended the stairs, Alyssa following with her head ducked.

"Allow me to introduce you to Luc Trahan."

Jackson took the man's hand. "Pleasure to meet you."

"Likewise." Luc had a sincerity about him, yet he also seemed to be sizing up Jackson.

Alyssa stood beside her sister. "Good morning."

Her voice sounded as beautiful to Jackson as the final

chorus of "Amazing Grace." He steeled his thoughts. "Morning, Alyssa."

CoCo's attention darted between them while the silence hung in the sharp air. "Mr. Devereaux, our grandmother is coming home from the hospital this afternoon. We're planning a late celebratory lunch around two. I wonder if you'd like to join us."

What could he say? Alyssa stared at him with those solemn eyes of hers, and he was sunk. Done for. Over and out.

"That'll give me plenty of time to go to the hospital and visit Bubba for a while, so sure, I'd love to. Can I bring anything?"

"Not a thing. Just yourself." CoCo looped her hand through the crook at Luc's elbow. "We'll see you at two, then."

He nodded, but his gaze rested on Alyssa. CoCo and Luc wandered toward the parking lot. Alyssa gave a shrug. "If you don't want to come, we understand."

What? And not be in her presence? Was she joking?

"No, I'm looking forward to it." Alyssa raised her eyebrow, so he backpedaled. He patted his flat stomach. "Been a while since I had a home-cooked meal."

A flash of something akin to disappointment flared in her eyes. "Then you're in for a treat. CoCo's one of the best cooks in the parish." She marched to her sister's vehicle.

What was that all about? Jackson moved to his truck, pondering what had caused Alyssa's shortness. He slammed the door and started the engine.

Now, more than ever, he needed to get into his Bible and listen to God.

TEN

The smoke alarm sounded with an eardrum-splitting shriek.

Smoke puffed out of the oven. Boiling water spilled over the pot, sloshing onto the stove's electric burner and sizzling.

Tears welled in Alyssa's eyes as she twisted the knob to turn the burner down on the stove. Why couldn't she do something as simple as boiling the pasta and keeping an eye on the bread without turning the kitchen into a danger zone?

Tara rushed into the kitchen, grabbed a pot holder, opened the oven door, then yanked the baking stone free to set on the counter. She closed the oven with her hip. "Good gravy, Al, can't you tell when bread's burning?"

Sure enough, the garlic-cheese loaves were a crunchy shade of black. Scorched and seared beyond redemption. Just like her ego.

"I told CoCo I couldn't cook," Alyssa hollered. The constant shrill beeping ripped against her mind.

Shaking her head, Tara grabbed the trash can and tossed the bread inside. "She didn't ask you to cook—she just asked you to take the bread out of the oven and keep an eye on the pasta." She leaned over and peeked into the bubbling pot. "I think the pasta's okay. Salvageable, anyway."

"Can I be of any help?" a deep voice asked from the kitchen doorway.

Alyssa dropped the glass lid to the spaghetti sauce jar. The top cracked, shattered shards pirouetting across the floor.

Jackson lifted his hands in front of him. "Sorry, I didn't mean to startle you."

"Can you get that thing to shut up?" Tara jerked her head toward the hallway.

He disappeared while Alyssa grabbed the broom and dustpan. "You could've mentioned our guest was here," she whispered to her sister as she bent and passed the broom over the floor.

Taking the spoon and stirring the simmering sauce, Tara shrugged. "He knocked on the door. Guess you couldn't have heard him over the smoke alarm."

Which, blessedly, went silent at that moment.

Her baby sister pulled two more loaves of bread from the freezer, cut them open and laid them on the baking stone. She set the oven's timer before putting them under the broiler.

Jackson returned as Alyssa emptied the glass into the trash. "I took the battery out."

Tara laid the back of her hand against her forehead in an exaggerated gesture. "My hero." She giggled and straightened, then threw a scathing glare at Alyssa. "I'm going to get Grandmere's chair ready before they get here. Try not to burn the bread this time." As she passed Jackson, she added in a stage whisper, "If the timer goes off, save the bread from Emeril there, okay?"

Heat crept up Alyssa's neck and into her cheeks, and not because of the over-warm temperature in the kitchen. Jackson stared at her with such pity in his eyes. Now her humiliation was complete. Perfect.

"Can I help with anything else?" At least he didn't smile like an indulgent parent to a pouting toddler.

"Don't want to leave me alone to burn more bread?"

He locked his gaze on hers, as if trying to gauge her mood. Actually, that should've been pretty simple to do—she hovered as near to boiling as the pasta pot.

"Can I put ice in the glasses or something?"

Could he really be that dense? Probably not. Most likely, his charm worked to worm his way out of sticky situations. At least he didn't dignify her question with an answer. "Sure."

He moved with the grace of being comfortable in a kitchen. Figured. He fit into any given situation. Like at the *Times-Picayune.*

Gravel crunched in the driveway, followed by a horn honking.

"They're here." Alyssa grabbed the stacks of plates and carried them to the kitchen table. She glanced out the window. Luc and CoCo assisted Grandmere from the Jeep.

Her grandmother looked better, less fragile than in the hospital. Maybe CoCo'd been right and the doctors here knew something about medicine. Still, Alyssa planned to watch Grandmere and call a cardiologist in Shreveport at the first sign of trouble.

"Welcome home, Grandmere," Tara shouted from the front door.

Alyssa bit back a groan and moved into the doorway. "Give her some room, Tara."

Her younger sister rolled her eyes and pushed open the screen door. Grandmere had no sooner crossed the threshold than Tara engulfed her in a hug. "Oh, I missed you."

"I missed you, too, *ma chère.*" Grandmere released Tara and hobbled farther into the house. "My, but it's good to be home." Her gaze danced to Alyssa. "I'm glad you're still here, *ma chère.*"

"Of course I'm still here, Grandmere." She leaned and planted a kiss on her grandmother's cheek. "I wouldn't leave until I knew you were okay."

As the words came out of her mouth, she realized they were one hundred percent true. Despite all she hated about Lagniappe and all she'd suffered over her grandmother's profession, she loved Grandmere more than anyone else. Sad that it had taken this situation to make her realize where her heart belonged.

Grandmere smiled knowingly, as if she understood the reckoning Alyssa had just uncovered. "What you got cooking, girl?"

Naturally, her grandmother would look straight at her. The smell of burnt bread still perfumed the air.

"Spaghetti and bread, if Alyssa didn't mess it up again," Tara interjected.

Alyssa wanted to throttle her. Seriously hurt her baby sister.

"And who's this handsome young man?"

Jackson extended his hand, took Grandmere's and planted a kiss over her knuckles. "Jackson Devereaux at your service, Mrs. LeBlanc."

"Oh, my. You're as handsome as my Marcel, Mr. Devereaux, back in the day."

"Let's get to the table, Grandmere," CoCo said as their grandmother's eyes shifted into that long-ago-vacant look.

Jackson brought the glasses while Alyssa helped Grandmere into the chair at the head of the table, opposite the window. CoCo and Luc worked side by side in bringing the pasta and sauce, while Tara turned off the timer and pulled the bread from the oven.

Once they were all seated, Luc cleared his throat. "May I bless the food, Mrs. LeBlanc?"

Grandmere hesitated only a second before slightly tilting her head.

Luc's deep voice offered up thanks for the food, for Grandmere's recovering health and for the importance of fellowship among loved ones. Alyssa struggled not to recall Luc worshipping strangely this morning alongside CoCo, his hands raised along with his voice.

As they passed bowls and piled plates to heaping, Alyssa noticed Jackson's continuing stare. Heat rose up her neck all over again. But in a good way.

"How's the sheriff today, Mr. Devereaux?" CoCo asked.

"The same."

"I went by and saw him this morning before church." Luc broke a piece of bread from the loaf. "The nurses said there's been no change. The doctors don't seem too optimistic."

Jackson stared at his plate. "I'm praying for a miracle."

"We're all praying for one." CoCo laid her hand over his.

Alyssa thought she caught a glimpse of tears in Jackson's eyes.

Why did he have to be so interesting? He could penetrate deep into the dark recesses of her spirit, to the point where she wanted to share all her secrets with him. She gave herself a mental shake. He was her competition. The man who held *her* job. She'd do well to remember that.

If only her fickle heart would pay attention.

The celebratory luncheon had been a smashing success. At least, that's how Jackson saw it. Alyssa's grandmother, a charming lady, kept the conversation lively with amusing tales from her hospital stay. Yet, he'd noticed Alyssa's intentional, not-so-subtle avoidance of his gaze. What could be going on in that head of hers?

After the meal, Tara escorted Mrs. LeBlanc to her room to rest. That Tara, she certainly was a handful. Full of mischievousness but with an intelligent wit beyond her years, she made Jackson laugh. Now that they'd washed the dishes, and Tara had gone to work, he sat on the front porch with Alyssa, CoCo and Luc.

A gentle breeze rustled the hydrangea bushes lining the front flower beds, lifting the hint of magnolias and swamp water. Smelled like home to Jackson. He glanced over to CoCo and Luc snuggling in the double swing. His heart twisted. A longing for something similar pressed against his chest, suffocating him. He forced himself to look away. Jackson Devereaux wasn't the type of man to want a happily ever after. No, siree. He wanted to be free as the wind picking up over the bayou. Free to follow any breaking story happening anywhere in the world.

"How's your little sister, Luc?" Alyssa asked.

"Doing great. Felicia's beau finally popped the question a few weeks ago."

"Really?" She faced Jackson. "Felicia has cerebral palsy and is confined to a wheelchair." She brushed the jagged bangs from her eyes. "Who's the lucky man?"

"Frank Thibodeaux. He's somewhat immature, but I think he genuinely loves Fel." Luc's expression bespoke of his seriousness in protecting his sister. "A couple of years ago, his uncle got him a job that pays well."

Jackson nearly swallowed his tongue. Lucky for him, no one seemed to notice his recognition of the name.

"Must be a good man for Felicia to love him." Alyssa's voice took on an almost wistful tone.

"I hope so." Luc laced his fingers with CoCo's. "Love can make an ordinary man do extraordinary things."

CoCo's blush caused Jackson to look away. Discomfort wove around him over witnessing such pure and unselfish love.

"I'd heard he was a suspect in your grandfather's murder. For a time," Alyssa said.

Luc nodded, pain etching deep into his face. "As were many of us."

"I need to make my afternoon run before Grandmere gets up." CoCo stood and stretched before smiling down at her boyfriend. "Want to go with?"

"*Oui,* of course."

Again, their apparent affection made Jackson more than uncomfortable. He'd seen people in love before, why did this bother him so much now?

The couple headed to CoCo's airboat. Jackson turned to Alyssa. "Have you heard anything from the FBI?"

She snorted. "Of course not. Like they'd tell me anything."

He didn't reply, instead, he watched CoCo and Luc in the boat. Luc planted a kiss against CoCo's temple, and the two seemed to lose themselves in each other's gaze.

"How long do you think it'll be before he pops the question?"

"What?"

He nodded toward the couple backing away in the boat. "Luc. How long do you think it'll be before he proposes to your sister?"

"I—I…hmm. I guess I never really thought about it. They were engaged before and just got back together a couple of months ago. It'll probably take some time."

"If the looks they were throwing each other are any indication, I'd bet she'll be sporting an engagement ring by Christmas."

She dusted her hands on her slacks. "Have you given any thought to those numbers on the cloth?"

She could jump from one subject to the other so fast, he needed a map to keep up.

"I've ruled out dates and times, based on the times Bubba noted he'd found the money." He pushed to his feet and leaned against the porch railing. "I still think we need to figure out who were the two deputies working the case."

"Too bad we don't have any *ins* on the force."

An image danced in front of his mind's eye. Platinum blonde. Early thirties. Gum popping. *Very* interested looks in his direction.

Missy.

"Well, I might be able to rustle up someone."

Alyssa tilted her head and stared at him. The sun caught the golden highlights in her crown, creating an aurora. Something in his gut tightened. Sure wasn't the spicy spaghetti from lunch.

"Who?"

"What?" He'd forgotten what they were talking about.

"Someone, who?" Alyssa put her hands on her hips.

"The dispatcher. Missy."

"The woman who couldn't stop staring at you?"

He swallowed the satisfying grin. Could that be jealousy he detected? "Yeah. I think maybe she could be our *in*."

Her nostrils flared.

She *was* jealous. "I figure if I ask her out to lunch or something, she might be more apt to fill me in on some juicy details of the case." He crossed his ankles and wrapped an arm around the porch post. "Everybody needs to eat and it'd get her out of the office."

She snorted and chewed on her bottom lip, right above that little mark.

At this close range, the dot looked like a burn mark. Surely not.

"Maybe." She spoke low, as if talking to herself.

Did he dare to think her truly disappointed?

"I feel useless just sitting around here waiting," she said.

"Why don't you look on the Internet and see if you can find a program for codes or something. Maybe we can figure out what those numbers mean."

"I suppose."

Jackson fought the urge to lean over and graze a kiss on her temple, much like Luc had done to CoCo. He needed to get away from Alyssa—clear his thoughts before he did something stupid, like show his attraction when he wasn't sure of her spiritual status. Besides, all her signals made it clear she wasn't interested in him.

The realization left him cold.

ELEVEN

Monday mornings were high on the list of things Alyssa would like to eliminate from the world. This Monday was no different. She'd gotten a run in her stocking when she'd stopped at the only gas station in Lagniappe. Knowing she couldn't show up at the senator's house with marred stockings, she'd run into the little grocery store to buy another pair, only to find they didn't carry her brand. What she wouldn't do for a Dillard's.

Changing into the off-brand hose in the small bathroom stall at the convenience store, she'd hopped on one foot and snapped the heel off her black pumps. About to cry over fate's laughter at her predicament, Alyssa remembered the pair of gray heels in her trunk. Sure, they pinched her toes and threw her off balance, but at least they'd match her suit skirt.

She'd awoke from another nightmare this morning. This time, of the crash itself. Were her dreams regressing? They'd started as soon as she'd returned to Lagniappe, but seemed to be moving backward in time. First waking up in the hospital. Then, being burned and in the car. Now, the crash itself. What could they mean?

Finally presentable enough for her personal satisfaction, Alyssa jerked the Honda in gear and gunned the engine, keeping an eye on the digital dashboard clock. She would not—could not—be late. Alyssa pressed the accelerator harder, peering at street signs. Come on, LaRue Avenue.

Flashing red and blue lights filled her rearview mirror. The piercing wail of a siren followed.

Great. Now she *would* be late to her interview. Mondays were the pits. She made a mental note to herself—never schedule interviews on Mondays from here on out.

She pulled over to the shoulder, if the space could be called such, and slammed into Park, all the while watching the officer get out of his cruiser and saunter toward her door. She rolled down her window as he approached.

Hurry up. Just write me the ticket and be done. Let me get on my way.

Deputy Anderson rested his arm against the roof of the car over her window. "Well, hello there, Ms. LeBlanc."

Recalling Jackson's insinuation that the lawman might be interested in her, she plastered on a bright smile. Hey, two could play the flirt-with-the-nice-cop-to-get-info game. Now, what *was* his first name?

"Deputy." She nodded, making sure she used the Southern drawl she'd fought so hard to tone down. "Was I speeding?" She laid a hand against her chest.

Oh, somebody should give her an Academy Award.

He leaned closer to the window. "Why, yes, ma'am, you sure were. I clocked you doing sixty-four in a forty-five."

"Oh, my. I'm so sorry. I'm late for an appointment and didn't pay attention to my little speedometer thing."

Could she sound any more ditzy? Surely men didn't buy this ploy.

"I can understand that, ma'am." By the appreciative look in his eye, he did buy it. Hook, line and sinker.

Reel him in.

"I'm so sorry, Deputy. I promise to watch my speed from now on."

He straightened and paused. Deliberating whether to give her a ticket or let her go with a warning?

She smiled wider and batted her eyelashes.

Oh, man. She actually batted her lashes. How sickening.

"Okay, Ms. LeBlanc. You keep your speed down now, ya hear?"

"Oh, yes, sir. Certainly will."

He smiled, almost as if he didn't want to let her go.

She cut her gaze to the clock. She had a couple of minutes to spare.

"Deputy, how's the investigation going?"

"I can't really discuss that with you, ma'am."

"I understand. I'm just saying, I don't know why they called in those FBI agents. I'm sure the Lagniappe sheriff deputies could work the case just as well. Probably better."

"I'd have to agree with you there, ma'am. They aren't even interested in looking at the cases the sheriff worked on before the attack."

This was too easy.

"I figured as much. In my experience, those federal boys can't find their thumbs in the dark with a flashlight."

"You can say that again. I even showed them the evidence of one case we were working on together. Could be something big. Do you think they even cared?"

Alyssa's heart sped. She gripped the steering wheel to calm herself. "Really?" She shook her head, options running through her mind. "Maybe they didn't take the case seriously if it was just something you and the sheriff were working on alone."

"But it wasn't. Deputy Martin Gocheaux has been working it, too."

"Well, I don't know what to say. That's just wrong."

"Yes, ma'am." The radio on his belt squeaked before Missy's voice recited a series of numbers. "Well, that's my call." He knocked on the roof of the Honda. "You keep it under the speed limit, Ms. LeBlanc."

"Will do."

She watched in the side mirror until he buckled his seat belt, then she put the car in Drive and steered back onto the road. She might arrive at the senator's in time, but if not, she'd at least gotten the name of the other deputy the sheriff had shared information with on the case. Oh yeah, she was good. Alyssa spared a second to wonder how Jackson fared with the buxom blonde dispatcher.

A sourness coated the back of her throat. Why should she care who Jackson flirted with? She wouldn't allow herself to be attracted to the man who held her job. No. Not now.

Suddenly she felt that odd sensation of being watched. She glanced in the rearview mirror and saw nothing. Must just be her mind playing tricks on her.

Luck decided to smile on her. The next main street sign read LaRue Avenue. She flipped on her blinker and turned north on the paved road. The senator had told her to look for the white house on the right, that she couldn't miss it. A quarter of a mile down the road, she understood.

No other homes littered the perfectly manicured and fenced lawn of Senator Mouton's estate. A white plantation home with eight columns across the front sat back several hundred yards from the road. An archway over the gated entrance held a wrought-iron sign reading MOUTON. Nope, no chance she'd miss it.

She crept down the driveway, taking in the drooping live oak trees lining the way. Miniature rosebushes filled the distance between the trees, forming a greenery fence. Alyssa pulled into the circular drive. She straightened her skirt as she exited, grabbed her briefcase and headed up the massive brick steps.

The ornate wooden door swung open before she could ring the bell. A lanky man, resembling a black Ichabod Crane, bowed low. "Ms. LeBlanc?"

"Yes."

A butler. The Moutons had a real live butler. Unreal.

"Follow me, please."

The heels of her gray pumps tapped against the marble foyer. Sculptures sat on elaborately designed pedestals. Large arrangements of fresh flowers adorned a polished wood highboy.

Talk about living in high cotton. The Moutons must be neck-deep in the crop.

The butler opened French doors and waved her into a formal sitting room. "Please have a seat. The senator will be with you directly."

"Thank you," she uttered and stared at the beautiful leather furniture. Art pieces framed in gilded gold hung on all four walls. A wet bar sat in the corner closest to her. The snifters and tumblers were Waterford crystal.

Alyssa didn't dare sit for fear of smudging the cream leather sofa.

"Thank you for waiting."

"Senator Mouton. Thank you for seeing me." She offered her hand.

His handshake wasn't as soft as the politicians she knew.

"Please, have a seat. May I get you a drink?"

Gently perching on the edge of the sofa, Alyssa shook her head. "I'm fine, thank you."

"Hope you don't mind if I have one. It's been a long morning already." He moved to the bar and opened a brandy decanter. The strong, smooth aroma with a touch of alcohol danced on the air.

White at the temples, his hair had a nice blend of brown and gray throughout the rest. A neatly trimmed mustache lined his upper lip. Eyes as green as kudzu leaves nestled under bushy gray eyebrows.

He took the chair opposite the sofa, drink in hand. The kid leather rustled, even though he couldn't weigh more than one hundred and fifty pounds. Those bright eyes pierced her. "You look like your mother, did you know?"

Her heartbeat thudded into the back of her throat. "I've been told that before." She pressed her lips together, waiting for the professional instinct to take over. The mention of her mother threw her off.

Her hero.

She pulled out her recorder and pressed the Record button before setting it beside her. She grabbed her pen and notebook. "Senator Mouton, tell me how you feel about a candidate running against you in the upcoming election, when there hasn't been one for the past decade and then some."

"I'm proud to live in a country where the people have a choice. This is a prime example of opportunities presented to the public. I welcome the race."

"Rumor has it that this candidate, Mr. Lewis, is arming himself with slanderous information regarding your past political actions. Care to respond?"

His face twisted into a somber expression. "I've heard that, Ms. LeBlanc, and I have to tell you, it saddens me to think that anyone aspiring to a position to represent the people would resort to such low actions." He shook his head before he took another drink of his iceless brandy.

"Is there anything in your political past that could hurt you if made public knowledge?"

"Now if there was, do you really think I'd announce it in an interview, Ms. LeBlanc?" He chuckled, but the sound came out dry, devoid of humor. "Honestly, I think everyone has a skeleton or two in their personal closet. We're human. But using information in a manner to make yourself look better…well, that just says a lot about the person's character, doesn't it?"

She flipped through the notes she'd made during her research last night. "Mr. Lewis claimed in a parish paper that the port authority of the intercoastal port just miles from your own home is corrupt. He states, and I quote, 'Senator Mouton has allowed the port authority to become a good ol' boys' network, with total disregard for the laws of our federal government.' End quote." She paused for effect. "Would you like to respond?"

"It would seem Mr. Lewis doesn't have his facts straight. That's the problem with some aspiring politicians in today's society—they rely on rumors and listen to the gossip mills." He took a long sip of his drink. "There is no corruption of the port authority. In the last ninety days, an overseeing committee conducted an internal audit. They found no exception in the accounting that couldn't be traced back to plain human error."

Oh, he'd mastered the fine art of sidestepping. Then again, he'd had many years of practice.

"Do you have any parting comments for Mr. Lewis?"

"I wish him the best of luck in the election. I have no ill will toward the man—I welcome the challenge. It would be nice, however, to stick to the issues. Unemployment, lack of federal funding, our schools—things that are important to the voters in this district. These are what I'm focusing on, not trying to smear someone's reputation."

Alyssa turned off the recorder and slipped it, along with her notebook and pen, into her briefcase. She flashed a smile. "I really appreciate this, Senator."

"Anything for Claire's daughter." He finished off his drink. "You know, I really miss her. She was such a breath of fresh air during a trying time."

The knot in her stomach tightened. "Really?"

"Oh, yes." He stood, walked to the bar and poured himself another glass. "Claire was a go-getter. She didn't care about anything but getting to the truth. One of the best in the business I've ever seen." He faced her and took a long sip. "Must be hard for you, being in her field and having to live up to her reputation."

And not measuring up to her high standards. Isn't that what he meant?

Alyssa swallowed the bile scorching the back of her mouth. "She was a photojournalist. I'm an investigative reporter."

"Same difference. Both look to expose the truth, yes?"

Yes.

Would she ever be able to shed the weight of her mother's accomplishments?

When compared side by side, Missy couldn't hold Alyssa's pen.

Jackson sat across the table from the dispatcher, listening to her drone on and on about herself. The eleven o'clock lunch crowd apparently didn't swarm the diner, much to Jackson's disappointment. He'd have loved a distraction. So much for being nice and getting her out of the office.

"And you know I was crowned Ms. Lagniappe, right?" Missy shoved a French fry, drowned in ketchup, into her busy mouth.

"No, I wasn't aware."

She swallowed. Had she even bothered to chew her food? "Oh, yeah. Of course, that was many moons ago." She gave a slow wink.

Didn't the woman realize she'd passed the age of college coed pickup lines? He didn't think he'd be able to finish his Reuben sandwich. "So, how'd a beauty queen become a sheriff's dispatcher?" As much as she jabbered, if he could just get her on subject, surely she'd let some information loose.

Hopefully, information he could use.

"Oh. Well, back then we had a different sheriff, Roger Thibodeaux, who was a little sweet on me, if I do say so myself. Although he was much too old for my taste. I was only eighteen, you know." She patted her dull hair. "He asked me to apply for the job when it opened up. I did, and I got it."

"The rest is history?"

"Yeah. I miss ol' Roger, though. He was like a favorite uncle figure to me. He works over at the rice plant now."

Focus, woman.

"You must love working at the police station, being on the inside of everything."

Missy laughed, brass and phony. So unlike Alyssa's throaty chuckles. "Just like I imagine you do, being a big-time reporter and all."

"It has its moments." He rested his elbows on the table and leaned forward. "But this business with Bubba has me upset. Very." He lowered his brows.

"Me, too. Did you know that he asked me out once?"

If his friend regained consciousness, Jackson would have a serious talk with Bubba about his taste in women. Or lack thereof.

"I just don't get why the FBI haven't found out anything yet." He bit the bullet and reached across the table to lay his hand over hers. "It's frustrating."

"They're trying, I suppose. Like, they've been checking up on Bubba's hunting buddies." She laid her other hand atop his and squeezed. "So far, they all have alibis."

He resisted the urge to flinch from her calloused hands. "Surely they could find some of the open cases he was working on and see if there's a link?"

"To date, they haven't found anything really important." Missy leaned close. "They couldn't even figure out what happened to that missing evidence from storage."

"What missing evidence?"

"Apparently, the sheriff had recently gotten some evidence on a case he was working on, cash at that, and logged it into the storage area. The night he was attacked, the evidence disappeared from storage."

"Really?"

She nodded, her hairspray-plastered hair not moving. "And the FBI agents, cute as they are, didn't even realize it until this morning." She shook her head. "They haven't a clue."

TWELVE

"You'll have it today," Alyssa grated into the phone as she typed away on her laptop, clicking filling the room. "I'll get an interview with his opponent as soon as I can to get a rebuttal article."

"Good job, kiddo. If you can dig up and prove the allegation this Lewis is making about Mouton, I'll run it front page." Simon rarely made such declarations.

Despite the bitter taste in her mouth, Alyssa's heartbeat quickened. "I'm also working on another piece."

"Something hot, I hope. Don't want you wasting your time."

If she told her editor the truth, he'd blow her off again. She couldn't chance that. Not with Marlee nipping at her career's heels. "I'm actually working with a reporter from the *Times-Picayune* on a story."

"What reporter?"

"A Jackson Devereaux. Ever heard of him?"

"Have I ever, kid. He's got a nose for sniffing out scandals." Glee laced Simon's tone before he sobered. "Don't let him get the scoop on you about Mouton."

Jackson wouldn't do that. Would he? He *was*, first and foremost, a reporter.

"He doesn't even know I'm working the angle." She rolled her shoulders, pushing the tension into her lower back. "Besides, the senator hasn't granted anyone else an interview."

"Keep it that way, or your article will be just one of many."

A cardinal sin in the journalism business. Sometimes the industry slap wore her out.

"Sure, boss."

Simon let out a long breath. She could picture him, sitting at his desk, cigar burning in the ashtray while he gnawed on a ratty toothpick. In the years she'd worked at the Shreveport paper, she'd never seen him actually smoke the cigar burning continuously at his hand.

"And get that rebuttal interview with Lewis."

"I'm on it."

The phone connection broke. Alyssa clicked the phone off and went back to her laptop. She scanned the information she'd already written. After pulling up every available interview she could find on Senator Mouton, she realized none had been invited into the sanctuary of the Mouton home. Another edge to her article—the description of his personal space.

She opened her Internet browser and did a search on Warren Lewis, the upstart candidate opposing Senator Mouton. Within moments, she had his office phone number. She lifted the cordless and punched the series of seven digits. When she told the chipper woman her name and what she wanted, they put her right through to Mr. Lewis.

"Ms. LeBlanc, how nice to hear from you." His tone suggested his eagerness to talk to the press.

"Mr. Lewis, I've just concluded an interview with

Senator Mouton regarding the forthcoming election. I'd like to offer you the opportunity to respond."

"That old goat denying my accusations?"

She inhaled slowly. Old goat? Senator Mouton had been one of the speakers at her parents' funeral, giving a beautiful eulogy to her mother's memory. She didn't think him capable of being an old goat. Dirty politics at its best, and she didn't like Mr. Lewis's attitude. While she'd like to just hang up the phone, Simon's constant insistence of putting aside personal feelings drummed in her ears. She clutched the phone tighter. "I'd really like to meet with you and ask a few questions."

"Sure, come on down to campaign headquarters, and I'll answer any question that *cooyon* threw out."

She flinched. "What time is good for you?"

"Come by now. I'm curious to hear what he had to say."

Hadn't he heard that curiosity killed the cat?

"I'm on my way."

She hung up the phone and went back to her article. She gave it a final read-through, satisfied she'd painted a strong picture. Then she opened her e-mail program. She fired off a quick message to Simon, letting him know she would have a rebuttal interview available tomorrow, attached her article on the senator and hit Send. She shut her laptop and stood, stretching. Tension weighted every muscle in her back and shoulders.

Sometimes, her job wore her out. While she loved the written word and enjoyed the rush of scoping out a good story, the truth was that she'd become to be quite disenchanted with reporting itself and the politics of the industry.

Grabbing her briefcase, she headed out the front door toward her car. If only she could report the good side of things, the better view of people. But those types of feel-good stories didn't win awards.

Would the sun ever shine where her mother's shadow hovered? How had Claire LeBlanc done it? Portraying emotions on film, uncovering a wealth of injustice, and still beloved by all. Maybe Alyssa would never have what it took.

No, she wouldn't allow her thoughts to drag her down. She would succeed—she'd worked too hard not to.

The noonday sun blazed in the sky, as Alyssa steered her car toward downtown Lagniappe. She flipped on the vent, only to be blasted by warm air. Ugh. The swampland coated the area in heat and mugginess. She pressed the button to turn on the air conditioner.

After parking in front of the strip center, which housed the temporary campaign office for Warren Lewis, Alyssa straightened her skirt, grabbed her briefcase and strode purposefully to the door. A gust of cool air greeted her.

About ten people were packed into the small space. If she did have claustrophobia, this place would send her into a tailspin. A middle-aged woman sitting at a desk answered the phone. A stack of old textbooks filled the gap for a missing leg on a battered desk. Two banquet-length folding tables filled the room, manned by people writing on posterboards or stuffing envelopes.

A young man stood. "Hi, there. How can we help you?"

"I'm looking for Warren Lewis. I'm Alyssa LeBlanc, here for an interview."

"Ah, you made it," said a booming voice from a door in the back of the room. "Come on back."

She wove around the table and desk, all the while taking stock of Mr. Lewis. Younger than Mouton by probably twenty years, Warren had the working-man look down pat. His hair had yet to be speckled by signs of graying. His skin had a sun-kissed glow, but its texture resembled worn leather. He wore blue jeans and a pullover. Nothing about his appearance set him apart from the rest of the workers.

Until she drew closer.

A long scar marred the entire left side of his face. Puckered and pink, but not recent. Alyssa knew the signs only too well. She rubbed her own scar, then stiffened her back and offered her hand. "Mr. Lewis."

"Thank you for coming down here so quickly. I appreciate it." He waved her toward the doorway. "Let's talk in my office."

An office? The room he indicated looked no bigger than a walk-in closet. A shabby desk sat against a wall, with two facing chairs. At least the desk had all four legs. He motioned her to sit. "Sorry it's not as nice as where Mouton held his interview, but I'm a working man. No silver spoon ever passed my lips."

She refrained from commenting. What could she say? This place couldn't even compare with the trash bin at the Mouton estate. She dropped into one of the chairs. The wood creaked in protest. Alyssa scooted closer to the edge of the seat.

Mr. Lewis took the other chair and slapped his thigh. "So, what'd old Mouton have to say about me now?"

She'd learned early in her reporting career not to allow herself to be badgered, but to take control of each and every interview. She placed her tape recorder on the edge of the desk while settling her notebook in her lap. Pen poised, Alyssa smiled. "Let's start at the beginning, shall we?" Without waiting for an answer, she plunged ahead with the questions she'd already formed. "What made you decide to run for senator, Mr. Lewis? Especially against such a popular incumbent?"

"I didn't like the way Mouton did the job. I uncovered some discrepancies in his actions. When I called him on them, he blew me off. That told me right then and there the man had something to hide."

"What sort of discrepancies?"

"Little things at first. Like unqualified people getting jobs over better-suited candidates."

"But that happens all the time, Mr. Lewis."

"Not as consistently as with Mouton. And his committees. He appointed people who had no clue. They did what he told them. Pigeons, that's what they are."

"Isn't that the function of a committee? To carry out the wishes of the person overseeing it?"

"Not like this. For instance, I found out some shipments left the port without going through an inspection. That's against federal guidelines for intercoastal ports. When I brought the situation into the open, Mouton formed an overseeing committee to audit the inspectors' books."

"Doesn't that imply he was concerned about the allegations and set out to research the facts?"

Mr. Lewis snorted. "His so-called committee consisted of one of the rice plant managers, a deputy and a dock manager—all Mouton flunkies. I'd hardly call that being concerned."

"But did this committee find any basis for your allegations?"

"You don't get it, Ms. LeBlanc. Those were all people on Mouton's payroll. Of course they didn't find anything amiss."

"Are you implying Senator Mouton instructed the members of the committee to look the other way with regard to federal guidelines?"

"I'm not implying it, Ms. LeBlanc. I'm out-and-out stating it."

Alyssa took a moment to gather her thoughts. "If what you say is true, what could possibly be the reason?"

"That's what I don't know. Why I'm running to find out. Something's going on out there at the port, right under the authorities' noses, and Mouton's got people covering it up."

"What's the benefit of shipments not going through inspections?"

"Lots of reasons. The load is heavier than the bill of lading declares, which would be more freight cost. Shipments not containing what they've listed on the sheets. Could be a number of things."

This man was adamant, and in a strange way, he made sense. But for Senator Mouton to be involved? The facts and the man who'd given such a moving speech at her parents' funeral didn't compute.

Time to change tactics.

"How'd you get that scar, Mr. Lewis?"

He hesitated, absently running a finger along the jagged skin. A habit Alyssa herself employed.

"I got mugged. This was the result."

"I'm so sorry." And she truly meant it. She hated using shock tactics, but she had a job to do. "I would think you'd be campaigning more on a platform of crime."

His smile turned into a sneer. "In a way, I am. You see,

Ms. LeBlanc, I was assaulted four years ago. Back when I began asking questions about what was going on."

What could she be doing in town?

Jackson paused at his truck, watching Alyssa stride to her Honda across the street. She'd come out of one of those holes-in-the-wall. What was she up to?

And why did she look so good?

He chewed his bottom lip and narrowed his eyes. She carried a briefcase and wore a straight skirt and blouse. Her short hair glistened in the sun. She must use that gel that made hair look wet even when dry.

Enough wondering. Jackson made clean steps across the parking lot to her car. She caught sight of him before he reached her. She tossed her briefcase into the passenger's seat and turned to face him. "How'd your date with Missy go?"

Ah, the green-eyed monster did stir within her. How promising.

"Just fine." He wouldn't let her know that the woman bored him beyond tears. "What're you doing in town?"

Her gaze darted to the building, then back to him quicker than a tornado could spin. "I had an errand to run. Did you find out anything interesting?"

So she wanted to play the avoidance game, did she? Okay. "Actually, I did."

"Do tell." Sauciness dripped from her words. "I found out something, too."

"Really?"

"Yep. From Deputy Anderson."

My, she had been busy today.

"Have you had lunch yet?"

"What?"

"Lunch? You know, one of the three squares, commonly eaten around now."

"I know what it means. No, I haven't."

"Let's grab a bite and update one another on our findings."

She nodded. "Where?"

He gestured toward the little diner sitting at the end of the town square. "How about there?"

"Sounds good."

"Want to walk?"

She rubbed that spot under her lip. "It's awfully sticky out."

"Come on." He took a gentle hold of her elbow. "Where's your sense of adventure?"

"Back in the air-conditioning," she mumbled as she shut and locked her car.

He noticed her walking with a bit of hesitation. Not a limp exactly, more like when he'd bought a new pair of shoes and wore them without breaking them in slowly. She wore fancy pointy-toed heels.

"Are your shoes hurting your feet?" he blurted out.

She faltered, but recovered quickly. "Why would you ask such a thing?"

Answering a question with a question—bull's-eye.

"You're walking funny."

Alyssa stiffened under his touch and jerked her arm free from his grasp. "I am not. I'm just trying to be more dignified than your strut."

Strut?

"Men don't strut, *chère,* they saunter. Watch your verb usage."

"Oh, please. Must you be so annoying?"

"Must you be so amusing?"

Her lips formed a tight line.

He focused on that little circle. "Is that a birthmark?"

She snapped her gaze to his. "What?"

Heat fanned his face. Had he really asked that aloud? How incredibly rude, but the question couldn't be un-asked now.

"That pink circle beneath your lip."

Her face lost all expression and her hand immediately went to the mark. She widened her eyes. Her nostrils flared. "It's a scar, not that it's any of your business."

Now he felt lower than the bottom of a quicksand pit. "I'm sorry."

"Don't be. Wasn't your fault." Her steps punctuated her words. Sharp. Curt. Precise.

They'd almost reached the diner's front door when guilt assailed him. He took her hand and jerked her back toward him.

She glared openly. "What?"

"A scar from what?"

"It's none of your business."

"But it's attractive, it draws my attention, and I want to know." Had he really just said that?

A myriad of emotions crossed her face, seeming to battle for dominance. Finally, dejection appeared to win. "A car accident when I was a young teen. A piece of hot metal adhered itself to my lip."

"I'm so sorry, Alyssa. Was anyone else hurt?"

Tears welled in her round eyes, twisting his gut.

"They were killed."

THIRTEEN

And I lived.

Alyssa jerked her arm free from Jackson's gentle grasp and stomped into the diner. She blinked furiously, as if that could whisk away the tears pooling in her eyes. No matter how many times she thought about the accident, guilt always won over logic. No matter that she'd been so young and unable to understand what happened. She'd lived, and they hadn't.

And had left her to the mercy of the small-minded townsfolk of Lagniappe.

The penetrating odor of grease and French fries nearly made her gag. Informality reigned the diner, no hostess to speak of, so Alyssa marched to a corner booth and slid in. She breathed through her mouth, nice and slow like the therapist had taught her. In and out. Smooth and steady.

Jackson sat silently across the table, his stare piercing the distance between them. She kept her head ducked, refusing to meet his eyes. How could she? She already knew there'd be either pity or condemnation reflected there—neither of which could she tolerate. Not from him.

"Do y'all know what you want?" a woman's voice asked, sounding tired and cranky.

The waitress took their order of cheeseburgers with fries and shuffled away. Alyssa met Jackson's inquiring look. At least he hid the compassion or censure. "I don't want to discuss it, okay?"

"I understand."

No, he didn't. He couldn't. But it was enough that he'd leave the subject alone.

He wiped invisible crumbs from the table. "Well, I found out something new on the case."

She arched a single brow, relieved he changed the topic so quickly.

"According to our friendly dispatcher, the day Bubba was attacked, some police evidence came up missing from their storage."

The case grew more intriguing with every turn.

"Did Ms. Flirt happen to say what particular evidence is missing?"

"Money from one of the cases Bubba worked."

"Have they recovered it?"

"Apparently not." He traced the grooves in the table with his thumb. "According to Missy, the FBI agents aren't overly concerned."

"Huh. Since it was money, you'd think they'd be a little more interested."

"You'd think. Obviously, someone on the force is involved with this case. I couldn't think of a way to get any more from Missy."

"Oh, I got the names of the deputies who were assigned to the case."

His mouth hung open, and his eyes widened.

She couldn't help herself, she chuckled aloud at his expression. "Well, if you can dig for info, so can I."

"How?"

"All because of my lead foot."

His eyes darkened in confusion.

"I got stopped for speeding by none other than Deputy Anderson."

He smiled, kicking himself mentally for not having caught on to what she'd said immediately. "And you flirted?"

"Of course not." She giggled. "Well, just a little bit. I'm really shocked men fall for such obvious ploys, by the way."

"I bet." His lips formed a hard line.

"Anyway, he and Martin Gocheaux were assigned to the case."

"Ring any bells?" he asked.

"Not off the top of my head, no. Remember, I haven't lived here in a long time and haven't visited in awhile." She shrugged. "And when I did visit, they were normally quick trips and I didn't pay much attention to anything going on locally." Truth be told, she hadn't paid much attention to anything.

"Well, the FBI aren't looking into the sheriff's open cases."

"Figures."

The waitress returned, plopped their plates and glasses on the table, and then spun away.

"So much for service with a smile," Jackson muttered.

"You know," Alyssa said as she lifted the pepper and dumped a smattering over her fries and burger, "one of those deputies has to be involved. But which one?"

"We need the duty roster from Friday night. That would tell us who'd been on duty. Whichever one wasn't working is most likely the culprit."

She swallowed the fry she'd just chewed. "True, because there wouldn't have been time for the assailant to drive off and then run back to the station." Alyssa wiped her mouth. "I don't think it's Deputy Anderson."

"Because he likes you?"

She frowned. Where had that come from? "No, because I don't recognize his voice. And he'd been the deputy who arrived first on the scene. He wore his uniform, still clean. If he'd been one of the men who attacked Bubba, he wouldn't have appeared all neat and tidy. Not without changing and cleaning up first. There was a lot of blood on the sheriff." Suddenly, the ketchup didn't look so appealing.

"Good point, but we still need to confirm that with a look-see at the duty roster." He pulled out a BlackBerry and punched buttons.

"What are you doing?"

"Asking my friend with the FBI in New Orleans to run a check on this Gocheaux." He glanced at her, warming her to her toes. "What'd you say his first name was?"

"Martin."

"Right." He punched more keys. "And it won't hurt to find information on Gary Anderson, too."

Gary. She'd need to remember that in the future. Just in case.

Jackson slipped the gadget back into his pocket. "Are you done? I've got work tonight."

She glanced at the ketchup on her plate. "Yeah." She pushed back from the table and headed to the door.

He had to take full strides to keep up with her. "What are you going to do?"

"I'm going home to check on my grandmother, try and visit with my sisters a bit, and ignore this case for a while."

"Oh. Okay. I'm going to run by the hospital and check on Bubba before I head to the dock." He ran a hand over his hair.

Frustration evaporated only to be replaced by something else—something she didn't want to identify. Her fingers itched to touch his waves, just to see if they were as soft as they looked. "Is there any change in his condition?"

"Nothing yet. But I'm praying for that miracle of healing."

Alyssa gripped the keys harder. She needed to get away from Jackson Devereaux. He made her think things she had no business considering.

"Do you want me to call you later and let you know what I find out, *chère?*" His voice came out more like a physical caress than mere words. Combined with the term of endearment, well, her heart fluttered.

"Yeah. Let me know." She opened her car door and dropped behind the steering wheel. Giving Jackson a quick smile, she started the engine.

Oh, yeah, she had to get away from him. He encompassed everything she wasn't looking for in a man—he'd taken a job that should have been hers, he had the arrogance of success, he carried himself with confidence.

Yet he had the softest expression in his eyes when he looked at her. Looked through her. Saw into her very soul.

Maybe the time had come to let the issue go. Wasn't his fault he won the job she'd wanted. All this time she'd spent coveting and resenting—wasted energy.

Well past time to let go of her animosity. But if she did, what would stop her from falling in love with Jackson Devereaux?

* * *

The sun descended behind the tips of the cypress trees surrounding the road to the intercoastal port. A hint of rain hung in the air.

Jackson whipped into the parking lot for the port employees and then made clean strides toward the men loitering around the dock.

Jackson kept track of each man's movements in his peripheral vision. The crew had accepted Burl's announcement of Jackson's temporary employment. No one seemed put out by his presence. Yet he could sense some leeriness lurking in a couple of the men's eyes. They watched him.

He'd gotten the rhythm of work flow quickly the last two shifts he'd worked. Trucks came in with loads to be shipped. Burl checked the paperwork, had the men open the crates and verified that the contents matched the listing in the bill of lading, then signed off on it. The men resealed the crates and loaded them on the boats designated. Pretty straightforward and routine. But Jackson kept track of every man's actions.

Another 18-wheeler backed up in a slot, its engine rumbling and smokestack polluting the air with exhaust. The foglike atmosphere blocked out the truck's logo on the side of the rig.

"Come help me with this one, Dawson," Burl ordered.

The young man dogging Burl's heels tossed off his work gloves and shuffled after the night manager. Burl turned and added, "You, too, Jax."

Jackson nodded to the man he'd been resealing crates with—Corey?—and followed the two men to the truck. The man Burl had addressed as Dawson stared at Jackson queerly. "Do I know you from somewhere?"

Great, just what he needed—to be recognized. Although he'd kept a pretty low profile since arriving in Lagniappe, this character might have seen him with Bubba. *That* wouldn't be good. "I don't think so. I'm from N'Awlins."

"Huh. You just look a little familiar."

Jackson turned away from Dawson.

The balding driver handed the paperwork to Burl. "Let's get this one done quickly. I've got a deadline to meet."

Dawson reached for the trailer's handle. At the driver's words, he stopped. He dropped his hands to his side and shifted his weight from one foot to the other.

Why wouldn't he open the doors and get busy?

Burl gave a curt jerk of his head. "Never mind, Jax. Dawson and I can handle this one ourselves."

What? The driver said he had a deadline. Two men working would be much faster than one. And just in the short period of his observations, he'd never call Dawson the quickest worker on the dock. Too slight and lacking in the muscles department to be much of an asset.

"Go on back to helping Corey." Burl's tone left no room for argument.

Jackson snuck a quick glance over the manager's shoulder before turning and heading back to the ship end of the port. He'd seen just enough of the bill of lading to confirm his suspicions that everything wasn't on the up-and-up.

Burl's signature was scrawled across the bottom of the bill. Yet he hadn't opened or inspected a single crate.

Back beside Corey, Jackson decided to take a risk. "Guess he just wanted me to walk across the dock for him," he muttered to his coworker.

Corey, with his smooth ebony skin, glanced over to the truck's slot. "Don't worry 'bout that, man. It's from the rice plant."

"So?"

"So, that's one of them shipments only Burl and Dawson inspect."

"Why's that?"

"I guess the owner only trusts them to do it right." He grinned and waggled his eyebrows. "Wouldn't do for us flunkies to mess up their precious rice cargo."

Very, very fascinating.

He needed a better look at that bill of lading. As he helped Corey load flats of crates to a ship, he kept glancing at Burl. The manager helped Dawson slip the truck's crates toward the ship docked next to the one where Jackson worked. First time he'd seen Burl do any physical work all night.

"Whew!" Corey said as he wiped his brow when they'd stored the last crate. "We can take a short break until the next truck comes." The tall black man's muscles rippled under his insulated undershirt.

"Should we help Burl and Dawson?" Jackson gestured toward the adjacent ship.

"No. I told you, they handle some shipments alone."

Jackson kept sneaking glances at Burl.

The men finished storing the crates. Dawson ambled back to the dock, while Burl locked and secured the ship, which he hadn't done for any of the other ships' cargos. Burl strode up to the clipboards where all the nightly bills were kept, slipped the paper to the bottom of the stack—not common procedure—then turned and headed to the truck.

Frank, standing near the paperwork, nodded discreetly to Jackson.

Now or never.

"I'm gonna run and use the facilities. I think I drank too much coffee," Jackson chuckled.

"Run on in, man. Burl'll be back in a few and will get us bustin' again."

Jackson forced his steps to be slow and steady when he really wanted to run and yank the clipboard off its rusty nail. He'd reached the end of the plank before Burl hollered at him.

"Where're ya goin', Jax?"

"Men's room. One too many coffees." He gave a forced laugh, hoping it sounded more casual to his boss than to his own ears.

"Hop to it. I need you to help load Steven's ship."

"Yes, sir." At the door to the office, he took a quick glance over his shoulder.

Burl stared at him from the end of the gangplank.

Jackson opened the door and stepped inside. He could grab his copies quickly, sure, but Burl might check up on him any second. He made his way down the hall to the men's room, forming a mental plan of attack. In the restroom he checked his BlackBerry for messages before washing his hands. He opened the door to find Burl filling the hallway.

"Sorry," Jackson said as he maneuvered around the manager.

"Didn't need to come here until you said something," Burl grumbled under his breath before shutting the door behind him.

His chance. Now.

Jackson snatched the copies and shoved them into his jacket, then trotted out of the office. His gaze darted about as he strode down the gangplank. Not a single man paid him any attention.

He grabbed the clipboard and flipped to the last page to stare at the bill of lading from the rice plant truck.

The paper reflected nothing but shipments of rice, scheduled to ship out of the port at four in the morning. Nothing unusual about that.

Jackson scanned the top of the bill, reflecting the shipper's name and address, the recipient's information, the date. And the shipment number—1022.

A four-digit code.

Just like the numbers scrawled on the pieces of cloth they'd found in the bayou.

FOURTEEN

*M*omee and Papa laughed softly in the front seat, their voices mingling to soothe her. Darkness surrounded the vehicle careening down the road to Lagniappe. She shifted to rest her head against the side window. Going to pick up her sisters. So tired from the interviews Momee had let her tag along to. Momee was so proud she wanted to go into journalism...following in Momee's line of work.

"What is that?" Papa exclaimed.

"Don't slow down, Robert." Momee's panicked tone heaved her upright.

Headlights pierced the shadows of the front windshield.

"They're coming straight for us."

"Don't stop the car."

Papa's face turned white in the glow of the console lights. "I have to, Claire, or we'll hit them head-on."

The car shuddered to a stop on the shoulder.

Momee glanced in the backseat. "It's okay, ma chère. Just sit tight. Keep your seat belt on."

She sat still, her stare not missing a thing in the front seat. Her hands trembled. She'd never seen Momee and Papa so anxious.

"They're coming straight for us, Claire."

"Do something, Robert!" Momee screamed.

Something cracked against the front windshield, shattering the glass. A ball of fire burst inside the car.

"They're going to kill us," Papa cried.

Metal crunched against metal.

The car spun around—almost in slow motion. She could make out the line of the trees and a big truck idling on the other side of the road. Colors blurred, blending together to form one big palette.

Round and round.

Flames licked the dashboard.

Momee screamed. Papa's hands gripped the steering wheel.

Another crash against the car. Metal ground.

Glass hit her face. Hot, searing pain under her lip.

Darkness.

Merciful darkness.

Alyssa bolted upright in the bed. Sweat coated her skin. Her hair plastered to her head. Her heart raced, pumping adrenaline through her veins. Every muscle was tensed and coiled. Her breath came in pants and gasps.

The dream again. Only, this time…this time her nightmare started in a place it never had previously. *Before* the crash. What did the timing mean?

Surrealism at its best.

She massaged the pounding of her temples and kicked her legs free of tangled sheets. Fighting to bring the dream into focus, she stumbled to the bathroom. The cold water splashed against her face helped clear her mind.

Staring at herself in the mirror, Alyssa organized the sequence of the dream.

The crash hadn't been an accident!

She ran back to her room, threw on a robe and flew down the stairs, nearly tripping in her haste. The rich aroma of coffee seeped into the hallway. Yes! CoCo would be up. Alyssa's heart thudded again, making every nerve tingle.

The uplifting yellow kitchen stood empty. Where could her sister be?

The bayou.

Shoving her feet into a pair of boots at the back door, Alyssa ran outside, toward where CoCo banked her airboat.

No boat, no CoCo. Not even a ripple in the murky water.

She had to tell somebody. Now. While the events remained fresh in her mind.

"Alyssa, *ma chère,* what are you doing out in your robe and those boots?"

She spun to face her grandmother, standing in the doorway of her work shed.

Yes! Someone who'd understand. She rushed to Grandmere's side. "I—I had…a dream. A-a-about the accident. Only…it wasn't an accident." Her words were as jumbled as her thoughts.

"Calm down, child." Grandmere wrapped a bony arm around Alyssa's shoulders. "Take it slow, *chère.* Catch your breath."

Her grandmother steered her into the shed and gently pushed her into a chair at the old wooden table. She thrust a glass of water into Alyssa's trembling hands. "Drink."

The glass shimmied against her teeth. Chills raced up and down her spine. She knew. She *knew.*

A hum rumbled from the bayou.

Grandmere glanced out the window. "Your sister's back from her morning run."

Good. She could tell both Grandmere and CoCo at the same time. She took another sip of the water. The liquid gurgled down to her stomach.

The drone of the boat's fan silenced. CoCo's cheerful voice drifted in the air. "Good morning, Grandmere."

"Come here, *ma chère*. Alyssa's here."

CoCo's lithe form filled the doorway. She took one glance at Alyssa and moved to kneel in front of her. "Al, what's wrong?"

Alyssa took a deep breath. She had to get the memory out without stammering. "I had a dream. About the accident."

"Oh, *Boo,* I'm sorry."

"No." She took another sip of water. "It was more than a dream. A memory."

"That's only natural, honey." CoCo clucked her tongue against the roof of her mouth. "Being back here—it probably brought up bad memories."

"Listen to me." She set the glass on the table with a jerk. Water sloshed over the rim. "I've had nightmares about the accident ever since it happened. This time was different. This time I remembered what happened *before* the crash."

Grandmere lowered herself into the other chair. "What, *chère?*"

"It wasn't an accident! I remember." She fought to even out her tone. "I remember being so sleepy in the backseat. Momee and Papa were laughing softly. Someone in another vehicle headed straight for us. Momee warned Papa not to stop. He said he had to, or we'd hit them head-on."

She focused on Grandmere's ashen face. "Something hit the windshield, which caused the fire. Papa tried to grab for me. Then something hit the car and spun us." She took a deep breath, her voice hiccuping. "Then the hot metal hit me, and everything went black." Alyssa rubbed her scar. The mark burned at the retelling.

"It's only a *cauchemar.*" CoCo shook her head and stared at her with sympathy oozing from her eyes.

"No, it's not just a dream. It was real. I remember!"

CoCo let out a soft sigh before glancing at Grandmere. Their grandmother wet her lips with the tip of her tongue. "I'll consult the spirits and see, *ma chère.*"

No! No! No!

"Grandmere—" CoCo started, but Alyssa interrupted. She jumped up, knocking over the chair. "That's all hocus-pocus, Grandmere. Smoke and mirrors." She banged her fist into her palm. "My dream was real. A memory."

"It was a nightmare, Al. A very bad one, that's all."

"It happened," Alyssa said through clenched teeth.

"No, sweetie. It's just your imagination in your subconscious."

"No, it's not. You don't know, CoCo. You weren't there. I was. And this is real." Tears trickled down her cheeks. "You might not be able to accept it, but I know the truth."

Fire flashed in CoCo's eyes. "What exactly are you saying?"

Alyssa pressed her back against the wall. "Momee and Papa didn't die in an accident. Make no mistake about it—someone murdered our parents. Deliberately and in cold blood."

* * *

Burl studied him like a fisherman watches a bobber.

Jackson finished his shift and loitered around the dock with the other workers. Unlike him, they kept a case of beer on ice in the back of their trucks. Several offered him a can, but he refused. Corey stared at him as if he'd just announced he came from Mars.

"You don't wanna drink, man?"

"I gave up drinking."

"What for?" Burl asked.

Jackson cut his gaze to the foreman. "Because I had a problem with it. I got stupid. I didn't know when to quit." He swallowed the rest of the truth.

"Ah, got busted and had to do rehab, huh?" Frank asked.

"Not exactly." More like, Bubba had saved his sorry self from a life of destruction.

Slipping into his truck, he offered up a prayer. He pulled into the hospital parking lot with his thoughts wandering to Alyssa. Where had she been all day? He'd tried to call her from the hospital before heading to the port, but got her voice mail. He'd left a message. When he'd phoned her house, her sister told him she wasn't home. All day, thoughts of her plagued him. Just the little things. Her smile. Her eyes. Her caring for Bubba.

Why hadn't she called back? Where'd she been all day?

He glanced at the digital clock's display. Too late to call her now. Maybe she'd return his messages in the morning.

The hospital's automatic doors whooshed open. Jackson stepped inside the cool foyer. No one sat behind the reception desk. He silently walked the hall to Bubba's room, nodding at the sole nurse working on the computer at the nurses' station.

"It's past visiting hours, Mr. Devereaux," she whispered.

"I'll only stay a few minutes. Just want to check on him before I hit the hay."

She smiled, winked and turned back to the computer.

He opened the door to Bubba's room. The machines hooked up to his friend emitted reassuring beeps. Jackson took Bubba's hand, his skin cold and clammy.

Jackson paused as his mind wrapped around the facts he'd learned.

God, help me find who did this to him and bring them to justice.

He stared at Bubba and wanted justice. Something fierce. Sure, life wasn't always fair, but this went beyond a promotion, raise or love.

"Pard, I sure wish you could open your eyes and give me some advice right now. I could use your insight." He snapped the sheets around Bubba. "You've always been a great adviser, directing me to Scripture to get my answer." He blinked away hot tears. "I'm praying for you. Praying for a miracle. Believing God will heal you."

The nurse slid open the door. "Mr. Devereaux, you'll have to leave now."

He patted his friend's hand, then leaned close to Bubba's ear to whisper. "I'm working on finding out who did this to you. Don't worry, I *will* expose those responsible."

Every time he sat with Bubba, the urge to find the men who'd done this to his friend nearly strangled him. He had to put all the pieces together. So close.

Starting with the shipment numbers. Those were key. He knew it—could feel the connection, even if he couldn't see one yet.

Once in his truck, he opened his BlackBerry and fired off a quick e-mail to his friend in the FBI.

ANY INFO GIVEN ON INTERCOASTAL PORT PAST ISSUES WOULD BE GREATLY APPRECIATED.

Jackson convinced himself he couldn't sleep after working, so he took the long way back to Bubba's house. Truth be told, he wanted to drive by the LeBlanc place. No reason for his actions. In the wee hours of the morning, everyone would be asleep. Yet something about the sadness in her voice when she'd shared the story about her scar had wrenched his heart.

But he'd detected more than sadness. He'd picked up on the pain and the guilt as well. While the urge to pry for more details pressed against him as oppressive as the humidity, the drive to comfort and help heal Alyssa tormented his spirit.

Accustomed to taking charge, swooping in and breaking a story to help fight for justice, Jackson couldn't reconcile himself to not being able to help.

Well, not yet. But he would. Once he found out the whole story.

And that would happen when he'd earned Alyssa's trust.

Knock. Knock. Knock.

Alyssa stood outside CoCo's bedroom, waiting. It was late evening, and light glowed from beneath the closed door. She held up her knuckles, prepared to knock again. Maybe her sister hadn't heard her.

Or maybe CoCo didn't want to talk to her. They didn't exactly part on good terms after CoCo hadn't believed her dream to be a suppressed memory—one that proved someone had murdered their parents. After not being able to convince CoCo of the truth, she'd gotten dressed and left. She'd spent an unproductive day at the library combing through old papers to find everything she could find on the death of her parents. It hadn't been an accident, and she needed to know their real fate. She'd just have to dig deeper. Find the connection.

Now she had to convince her sister.

She knocked again.

"Come in." CoCo's voice floated through the wooden door.

Alyssa poked her head in. CoCo sat on the bed, her Bible open in her lap. She smiled and shut the book. "How was your day?"

Her sister read the Bible outside of church?

Alyssa entered and sat on the edge of CoCo's bed. "Fine. I spent the day at the library."

"Doing what?"

"Reading everything I could about Momee and Papa's deaths."

CoCo set the Bible on her bedside table and sat crossed-legged. "I really wish you'd let this go, Al. The police concluded it was an accident."

"Caused by what?" Alyssa held up her hand when CoCo opened her mouth. "Think about it for a minute. What caused the accident? Papa was an excellent driver. He grew up on these roads—knew them like you know the alligators in the bayou." She ticked off items on her fingers. "They found nothing faulty with the car, not a single thing. So, you tell me—what caused the accident?"

"We'll never know for sure, *Boo,* but it's believed Papa

fell asleep at the wheel, hit the telephone pole and slammed into the tree."

"We *can* know, CoCo. That's just it. I was there. I remember. Papa wasn't asleep. He and Momee were laughing and talking."

"That's just your imagination."

"No, it's not." Although she spoke through clenched teeth, Alyssa didn't raise her voice.

"If that's true, why now? Why not have this recollection thirteen years ago? Ten years ago? It doesn't make sense for you to remember something after all these years."

"I don't know. Maybe because I'm back in the bayou. Maybe because I've been thinking about Momee a lot since I interviewed Senator Mouton, and he'd spoken at the funeral. Maybe because Jackson asked about my scar. I don't know." She shook her head. "I do know this isn't like the regular dreams—nightmares—I have about the wreck. This was different. This was a memory."

CoCo remained silent and pensive.

"I'm positive. I feel so strongly about this."

CoCo uncrossed her legs. "Then we need to take this to God."

"W-what?" Alyssa stammered. Had her sister gone off the deep end?

"Al, you do pray, right?"

"Of course I do." Sure she did. Thanking God for blessings, asking for protection. But to ask about a certain situation?

"I meant, do you take things to God on a daily basis? Before you make decisions?"

Oh, please. God had too much to deal with running the

world than to worry about each and every little issue that popped up. "No."

The saddest expression flickered in CoCo's eyes. "Honey, you don't have a personal relationship with God?"

A personal relationship with God? It's not like they went bowling together, no.

CoCo laid a hand over Alyssa's. "God is not only your heavenly Father, but also your best friend. He's there to listen, to advise, to hold you in His arms when that's all there is in this world that will give you peace."

Sounded more like a fairy godmother.

"First Peter 5, verse 7 tells us, 'Cast all your anxiety on Him because He cares for you.'" She smiled. "You can't get more clear than that."

The vision of her sister's face during church worship came to mind. "At church, you closed your eyes and lifted your arms during the music. Why?"

CoCo chuckled. "I feel so close to Him when I'm singing His praises. I close my eyes and lift my hands because my spirit leads me to do that. We all worship differently, Al. That's just how I feel led to praise Him."

Stated like that, the reason seemed…sane. Alyssa didn't even know why tears spilled from her eyes. Could she have a relationship like that with God? So personal?

As if she could read Alyssa's thoughts, CoCo stood and faced her. "He isn't some unapproachable God sitting up on clouds looking down on us. He's with us. Loving us. Picking us up when we fall. Listening to our heartfelt prayers."

Something to consider.

But…later.

Time to get the train back on track. "CoCo, I'm serious. Momee and Papa were murdered."

Her sister let out a sigh, accepting the change of subject. "If that's true, who? Why?"

"I don't know. I found some interesting articles in the papers that gave me some ideas." Alyssa shoved to her feet and paced the rug in front of CoCo's bed. "I intend to ferret out the truth."

"Is that smart?"

"Was it smart for you to expose Grandpere as a Klansman?" She raised a finger. "I'm not arguing that you shouldn't have. You had to do what was right." She ran her hands up and down her arms, fighting off the chill coming from within. "It's the same with this. I'll never have peace until I uncover the truth."

CoCo let out a long breath. "Where do we start?"

FIFTEEN

The sun wouldn't appear for another hour or so, but Alyssa couldn't sleep. She'd showered and dressed before stealing downstairs. She grabbed her keys and tiptoed to her car.

"Where're you going this early in the morning?" Tara asked from the edge of the driveway.

Alyssa jumped, jerking her hand over her thumping heart. "You scared me. What're you doing out here?"

"I just got home from work. What's your excuse?"

"I'm running out to Milo Point Road to check up on something."

"Before daylight?"

"By the time I get there, dawn should be breaking."

"Must be pretty important."

"It's for a story I'm working on." Alyssa studied her baby sister. Maybe they could connect somehow. "Would you like to ride with me?"

"I don't think so. I'm beat."

Oh, well. She'd tried. "Okay." Alyssa flashed a forced smile. "I'll see you later."

The drive took her longer than she anticipated. How had the route seemed quicker when she and CoCo had gone to church? Probably because it'd been daylight. No worries, though. Keeping the number on the speedometer well below the posted speed limit, Alyssa studied every street sign. She didn't want to miss the turnoff.

Finally, the rusty sign appeared. Dust rose as she turned onto Milo Point Road. The first rays of the sun cut against the darkened sky as the Honda rattled over the dirt road filled with potholes. She would get in and out of the bayou since she and CoCo had plans to do more research into the death of their parents. Starting with finding out what story her mother had been working on at the time of the accident.

Correction, the murder.

The dead end of Milo Point Road loomed just as CoCo had described. She parked, retrieving her flashlight, and locked the car. Alyssa tucked the legs of her jeans into the hiking boots CoCo had loaned her. Wandering around in the bayou wasn't her idea of fun, but she needed to know how quickly she could get to the location and back on foot to gauge how much time a pickup person would need to retrieve the money. She also wanted to see if there were any clues left along the way. She took note of the time on her watch and hiked on the path to the craggy outlying point.

The musty smell of the swamp filled her nostrils. She kept the flashlight beam directly on the way in front of her. Seeing a snake or one of the alligators CoCo kept track of would send her over the mental edge.

The trail narrowed, and the trees on either side drew denser. She nearly lost her footing twice. The trees closed in on her. The lushness of the foliage blocked out the sun. The footpath took sharp veers, as if whoever had cut it had intended the path to remain hidden.

Just when she wondered if she'd gotten turned around on the overgrown trail, she spied the bayou up ahead. Alyssa glanced at her watch—almost fifteen minutes had passed. Not too bad. If she'd been familiar with the place, the trek probably would've taken her less time.

She reached the edge of the swamp and stared at the little cove they'd visited in CoCo's boat. Alyssa estimated she'd have to add in another fifteen minutes to get there and back—she certainly wouldn't make a trip to get the actual time.

Just as she took a step to head back along the path, bushes shook to her right.

She flipped off the flashlight and dropped to her knees. An alligator? Some other creepy reptile? Alyssa lifted her head to peer at the bushes.

A man dressed in camouflage stood about two hundred feet away. Staring at her.

She swallowed a scream.

He moved toward her.

Running.

Adrenaline pushed her legs into action.

Alyssa swerved sharp right, dropping the flashlight. She headed down the path. Stumbled in her haste. Over-corrected. Regained her footing and continued running at top speed.

Overgrown and untamed, the bayou swallowed her into its depths as she fled. Cypress branches slapped her face as she ran down the trail. The hiking boots clamored against the uneven ground, rubbing against her heel.

Gasping as if someone had vacuumed the air from her lungs, she stopped and squatted behind a cluster of wild palmettos, listening…waiting. Only the blood pounding in her ears registered. Maybe he'd only wanted to frighten her and hadn't followed. She panted and willed her breathing capacity to increase before her next running jag. If she had to keep running.

The rustle of slapping trees erupted behind her. Oh, yeah, he'd followed her. She jumped and raced in the direction of her car, straying off the path. Her leg muscles burned as the bayou grabbed at her calves and thighs, as if she ran in quicksand. Swerving left, she ducked under a low-hanging limb. Spanish moss stuck in her hair, hanging over her eyes. She jerked the stringy lichen free and tossed it aside, her feet continuing to make tracks along the path.

Faster and faster she ran, in spite of nature's obstacles blocking her escape route. Mustiness with the underlying sweet aroma of onion flowers filled Alyssa's nostrils— or could that be the stench of her fear?

The thundering footsteps sounded close. Closer.

If she could just get to the car…

She wove to the right, leaping over two fallen oak trees. She landed with a thud. Jolts of pain shot up her left leg from her ankle. No time to check.

Keep running or die.

Hearing the ominous footfalls drawing closer, Alyssa bolted to her feet. Her left ankle gave, but her spirit refused to buckle. She had no other option *but* to run.

The crack of a gun firing resonated on the bayou. She ducked behind a palmetto, toppling face-first into the cool soil. Fire licked the muscles in her leg.

The fresh hint of ripe hackberries hung in the thick air, making her stomach churn even more. Alyssa's blood thrummed through her veins. Why had she come to the bayou? Alyssa bent her head to use the bush as cover. Maybe the man wouldn't see her.

Maybe she should do some praying. See if CoCo was right.

Please, let CoCo be right.

Dear God, keep me safe. Don't let him find me. Please, God.

She still hadn't returned his calls.

Jackson dialed Alyssa's cell phone, but the call went straight to voice mail. While it was early for some people, CoCo had told him she got up by six every morning to do her bayou run. Still, he didn't want to disturb Ms. LeBlanc since she'd just gotten home from the hospital. He glanced at the clock. After seven. Close enough. He dialed the LeBlanc home.

"Hello." The female voice wasn't Alyssa's.

Disappointment bombarded his heart.

"CoCo?"

"Nope, Tara. CoCo's out in her boat."

"Hi, Tara. This is Jackson Devereaux. I'm trying to get in touch with Alyssa. Is she still asleep?"

"No, she left early this morning. Before CoCo even."

Not good. "Do you know where she went?"

"She said she was going out to Milo Point Road. Research for some story she's working on."

Research? The only story she'd be working on involved Bubba's case. He reached for a pair of jeans. "Um, can you give me a general idea where Milo Point Road is?"

Tara laughed, throaty and full, reminding him of Alyssa's. His gut tightened, twisting. "It's north off Harden Lane, just outside the town limits."

"Thanks."

He ran to the truck, déjà vu washing over him. His heart pounded as hard as when he'd heard the call about Bubba.

Dear God, please keep Alyssa safe. Let me be wrong this time.

But deep inside, he knew. The prompting of the Holy Spirit burned the intensity into his soul.

He stepped on the gas pedal, and the truck threw gravel and dust in its wake. He knew the general area of Harden Lane, which ran through four parishes. He'd followed the same road on his way to church last Sunday.

His BlackBerry vibrated against his pocket. Maybe Alyssa calling. Steering with one hand, he grabbed the gadget and answered the call without glimpsing at the caller ID screen. Times like this made him wish he hadn't left his Bluetooth headset back in New Orleans. "Alyssa?"

"No, it's Brian."

"Now's really not a good time." Jackson watched for the city limits sign and tried to concentrate on what his friend from the FBI said.

Had Tara said near the city limits or outside?

"Just wanted to touch base. Gary Anderson doesn't have a thing on his record. Clean as a whistle."

"Okay."

"But that Martin Gocheaux? How he ever got on any police force is beyond me."

"He has a record?"

"Nothing ever proven. Never officially charged."

"But he was implicated?"

"A couple of illegal arms issues."

Yes! The city limits sign. Jackson took his foot off the gas pedal. "Thanks, buddy. Can you e-mail me that info?"

"Sure. Listen, the two agents down there are coming up empty-handed. Anything I can pass along their way?"

Jackson laughed, despite his mouth going dry. "That I'm not a suspect."

"I already did that, Jacks."

"Must be why they've left me alone the last couple of days." A street sign caught the sun's first rays.

"Be careful. They have a feeling an insider was involved."

"Took 'em long enough to figure that one out."

"Think it's this Gocheaux?"

"That's how I figure it."

"Hmm. Let me know when you get something concrete, okay?"

"Sure. Thanks, Brian."

Jackson dropped the BlackBerry into the truck's console. He made the turn onto Milo Point Road and accelerated again.

Please, God, keep her safe. Let me get to her in time.

He spied her car before he realized he'd reached a dead end. What could she be doing out here? The sun cast glares off her windshield. He parked the truck alongside her Honda, and leaped to the ground. The car sat locked up as usual, but Alyssa wasn't in sight.

Cupping his hands around his mouth, he hollered. "Alyssa. Alyssa."

He waited, measuring the silence. No birds chirped. No cicadas rasped. Odd out here in the bayou. Taking a slow turn, he studied the terrain. Woods…bushes…wait, could that be a trail? He moved closer. A path.

With impressions of fresh footprints. About Alyssa's size.

Jackson headed down the trail, studying the foliage as

he passed. A broken limb here, missing leaves there. Someone had definitely taken this route recently. He quickened his pace.

If his bearings were correct, which they normally were, and he kept on this trail, he'd run right into the swamp. Really close to the money drop site.

Energy zinged through his body. The trees closed in tighter around him. The upper limbs blocked out the sun's harsh rays.

"Alyssa. Alyssa."

He reached a sharp curve to the left.

A woman's scream pierced the air.

Not just any woman's—Alyssa's.

Not just any scream—one calling *his* name.

SIXTEEN

Jackson! Really here!

She'd heard him calling her name before, now again. Not her imagination or wishful thinking.

Alyssa crouched lower behind the palmetto, ignoring the prickling against her face. If she balled up small enough, the man chasing her wouldn't see her, and she'd be safe. She prayed Jackson would reach her first, if he didn't get himself shot.

"Alyssa!" By the sound of his voice, Jackson drew close.

But she could also hear the thrashing of bushes behind her drawing near, as well. She couldn't risk speaking—if her hearing could be trusted, the man chasing her was closer than Jackson.

Her pursuer crashed through the underbrush not more than four feet in front of her hiding spot. She bit her bottom lip, refusing to let the scream escape. The metallic taste of blood filled her mouth. She willed her body not to move even a fraction of a millimeter. Alyssa struggled to breathe through her nose, quietly.

He turned his head, looking into the trees and brambles. Then stared directly at her.

Her heart pounded. Surely he could hear the roar of the beating.

"Alyssa!"

The man jerked his head toward the path, and hesitated a moment. A second later, he disappeared back toward the bayou.

Jackson's tall form appeared on the trail.

Her hero!

"Jackson." Her voice cracked.

He ran to her, shoving aside branches and limbs.

She tried to stand, but her legs felt as if they were filled with grits. Hot pain shot up from her ankle.

Reaching her, Jackson drew her into his arms. Holding her. Comforting. Murmuring words of assurance as he kissed the crown of her head.

Warmth. Safety. Alyssa snuggled deeper against his muscular chest, ignoring the fear and pain.

"Are you okay? What happened?"

"Man…chasing me. He sh-shot at me."

"Someone shot at you?" Keeping her in his arms, Jackson spun around toward the path. "Where?"

"He ran off when you called my name." Saving her. Tears burned her eyes.

"Which way did he go?"

"Toward the bayou."

He released his hold. "Let me go check it out."

She gripped his shirt, crumpling the fabric in her fist. "Don't leave me. I hurt my ankle."

Jackson paused, as if arguing with himself. He pulled her back into his arms. "It's okay."

"Home. I want to go home."

He led her to the path. "Come on, *chère*. Let me get you out of here."

She limped, white-hot pain nearly forcing tears from her eyes.

"What happened?"

"I think I twisted it."

"Let me carry you."

Before she could argue, he lifted her smoothly into his arms. She felt so cared for, so fragile and delicate, and for once, she didn't care.

Her heart had returned to its normal beating by the time they reached the dead end. She breathed slowly.

"Let me drive you home. We can come back for your car later."

"No, I'm fine now. It's my left ankle that's hurt. I probably just sprained it." While the fear had subsided, questions now pervaded her mind. "I need to know who it was."

"Did you get a look at the guy?"

"Not really. He wore camouflage, saw me at the edge of the swamp and started chasing me." She rubbed her scar. "I didn't look back."

"Did he say anything?"

"No."

"Maybe it was just someone who thought you were trespassing."

She glared at him. "Shooting at me? I don't think so."

He leaned against the side of her car, studying her with an intensity stronger than the pain in her ankle. "What were you doing out here alone, anyway?"

"Following up on gaining access to the drop site by land."

"Why didn't you ask me to come with you?"

Because she wanted to find a clue herself. Prove to herself that she was just as good at investigating as him. "I didn't expect to be chased down or shot at." But something had changed inside her. She didn't feel the need to compete against him anymore.

Frustration oozed from his sigh. "*Chère,* you can't be running out alone and putting yourself in danger."

"Like you're not doing that working at the port?"

"I can handle it."

"And I can't?" She jerked open the car door. "Don't answer that."

"Come on, you're being prissy."

She dropped into the driver's seat. "Look, I thank you for coming to my rescue and all, but I'm fine. I'm not some delicate little female you have to take care of." *Unless some freak takes a shot at me in the bayou again.* Alyssa jammed the key into the ignition.

"I didn't imply that you were helpless." He ran a hand over his hair. "You scared me is all."

Guilt slammed against her heart. She softened her tone. "I'm sorry. Guess I'm still a little shaken up."

"Can I follow you home? There're a couple of things I'd like to share with you."

She nodded, the words not coming.

Her thoughts churned as she drove, careful to keep any pressure off her left ankle. Who'd been chasing her? Why'd he run after her? Why'd he shoot at her? She tapped her thumb against the steering wheel. His legs had been wet, she remembered that now. As if he'd been wading in the swamp.

Wading to the island to pick up dropped money?

* * *

Jackson accepted a refill of coffee from CoCo. He snuck another glance at Alyssa. She'd been the embodiment of composure when they'd returned to the LeBlanc home, relaying the events to her sister, then later to Deputy Anderson. An ice pack laid on her left ankle propped up in a chair.

"There shouldn't have been anyone out in that area of the bayou today." CoCo set the carafe back on the burner before joining them at the kitchen table. "I know the schedules for everyone working in this area."

"Well, I assure you, the man chasing me wasn't a figment of my imagination. Neither was the gunshot."

"I didn't say that, *Boo*."

"I think we can agree none of us should be out there alone from now on." Jackson watched the sisters' expressions change.

CoCo laughed. "That's my job. I'm alone on the bayou for several hours each day."

"Maybe you should ask Luc to assist you for a while." Didn't these women get that danger sat waiting for them?

"I'm quite capable of handling things myself."

"You could always sic a gator on them." Alyssa chuckled.

"Ladies, this isn't some game. This is serious. Somebody is intent on protecting their drug trade. Let me tell you what I found out at the port dock and from one of my sources."

Silence hung in the air when he finished.

Alyssa tapped her nails against the table. "So, the numbers on the cloths are shipment numbers?"

"Best I can tell."

"And this deputy has been implicated in crimes before?" CoCo asked.

"According to my source at the FBI."

Alyssa took a sip of her coffee. "We can assume Gocheaux is involved, but we can't prove anything yet."

"And we can guess the shipment numbers are what's written on those cloths, but until I can find the others, we have nothing to turn over to the FBI."

"What are you going to do?" CoCo included both of them in her question.

"Tonight, I'm going to get into the office. I'll try to find the other bills of lading and make copies. Maybe then we can prove the link."

"I'm going to talk to a source and see what I can find out about his mugging on the dock four years ago." Alyssa took a sip of her coffee.

"What source?" Jackson asked.

Alyssa let out a sigh. "Warren Lewis."

"The man running against Senator Mouton?" asked CoCo.

"Yep."

CoCo narrowed her eyes. "How do you know about the mugging?"

"I interviewed him." Alyssa rolled her eyes. "A piece my editor asked me to do for our paper."

"You do remember that Senator Mouton was a friend of Momee's, right? That he gave a moving eulogy at the funerals?"

"Yes. I interviewed him first. Lewis was just a rebuttal."

"You know, Lewis has been making all kinds of fuss about corruption at the port," CoCo said.

Wait a minute. Back the truck up. Jackson stared at Alyssa. "You got an interview with Mouton?"

"Yep." Her smile held a hint of victory. "It's in today's edition of my paper. The one on Lewis will run tomorrow."

Mouton didn't give interviews. Jackson knew first-hand—he'd requested one just last week and the Senator had declined. Jackson took a quick inventory of his emotions and surprised himself by not detecting a twinge of professional jealousy. Interesting. He usually did when another reporter got an exclusive he'd requested.

CoCo stood. "I have to do my run. Y'all be careful."

"Are we still going to the library this afternoon?"

"As soon as I get back."

The library? Jackson waited until CoCo had left. "What're you going to the library for?"

Alyssa's eyes hardened. "Personal stuff."

"At the library?"

"Let it go, Jackson." She hobbled to put her coffee cup in the sink, keeping her back to him. "Please."

That single word knotted his emotions. He shoved to his feet. "I'm going to the hospital to check on Bubba."

"Is there any change?"

"No. The doctors aren't very hopeful after he's been in a coma this long." His stomach churned. "I'm just praying God will heal him completely."

"I'm not sure I understand what you're getting at, Ms. LeBlanc." Warren Lewis stared at Alyssa with a hardness he hadn't exhibited in their previous interview.

"I think you do. You want someone to help you dig up the truth about the intercoastal port. I'm offering you that, but you have to be honest with me." She crossed her arms over her chest. "I need you to level with me here and now about what you think is going on."

He hesitated, rubbing his chin before letting out a sigh. "The last time I started the probe, I got assaulted. I don't want to cause harm to anyone else. If you start rattling the cages, there's no telling what beast you could awaken."

"I'll take my chances." She shifted to remove pressure off her ankle. She'd already rattled cages.

"And this is off the record, yes?"

"Of course. I told you this is just for my own information."

He tossed his pen onto the table. "Okay. I used to work with the former union administrator. Four years ago, I began investigating some rumors I'd heard regarding dealings going on out there on the dock."

"What kind of rumors?" Alyssa interrupted, jotting notes in her notebook.

"Rumors that some illegal smuggling took place. All regarding shipments coming out of the rice plant."

That jibed with what Jackson had told her.

Warren Lewis traced imaginary circles on the table. "Roger Thibodeaux is the rice plant manager. He's been there over ten years, after he retired from the sheriff's office."

As Missy had told Jackson.

"I'd heard that Roger ran a smuggling operation out of the rice plant through the port."

"What did you think they were smuggling?"

"Drugs, mostly."

"Did you ever find proof of that?"

"No. I even called DEA. They sent a team with a drug-sniffing dog. Stayed out on the docks for two weeks and never found anything, so they left."

"But you were convinced?"

He shook his head. "Not was…*am* still convinced. After DEA left, I asked more questions."

"Asked who?"

"Anybody. Everybody. I even confronted Roger Thibodeaux at Cajun's Wharf one night."

Alyssa glanced up from her note-taking. "How'd that turn out?"

"Not very well. He denied everything, of course. Told me I was off my rocker. Said I shouldn't stick my nose where it didn't belong." He steepled his hands over the table. "That's when I knew I was on the right track."

"So, what'd you do?"

"I switched my probing from the rice plant to the dock. One of the night managers, Burl somebody, threatened me if I didn't leave."

Burl. Jackson's boss.

Alyssa's heart hiccuped. "And did you?"

"I left that night. Drove back to Lagniappe. I stopped at the café to have a sip of coffee." He ran a finger over his pointed chin. "I was only there about twenty or thirty minutes before I headed home. The minute I stepped out of my car, someone assaulted me."

Her stomach twisted. "And you think it's because you were asking questions on the dock?"

"I'm positive. They never found my attacker. To tell the truth, I don't think they looked very hard. The officer who worked my case was the replacement Roger Thibodeaux named personally." He gave a snort. "You figure it out."

This sounded too close to home.

"So, you didn't follow up anymore?"

"For about two years, no. I focused on trying to heal and let it go."

"But now?"

"Now, I feel it's up to me to expose the truth."

"But you never found any proof of drug smuggling. Even with the DEA." She tapped the end of her pen against her notebook. "Is it possible, Mr. Lewis, that you're wrong? That there never has been any smuggling going on?"

"Anything's possible. But do I believe that? Not for a minute." He certainly sounded convinced.

"How does this tie with Senator Mouton?"

"The senator is over the port authority. He's overseen it for nearly two decades. When I started my own investigation, several staffers from his office called and ordered me to stop asking questions."

"Did they threaten you? Did you go to the police?"

He shook his head. "They didn't come right out and threaten me. More like an implied warning. And I didn't go to the police because, at that time, I had nothing to offer them."

"I see."

"When I finally became really vocal this past year about my investigation, Senator Mouton formed a committee to look into my allegations."

"And?"

"They found nothing. Big surprise."

"You don't think the senator is sincere about probing into the matter?"

"Not at all." He leaned forward, resting his elbows on the table. "The way I see it, the senator is involved in this smuggling up to his snobbish ears."

"How do you figure?"

"He's always had connections to the rice plant manager.

I've done some digging. Back before Roger Thibodeaux took over, Joey Blu had the position. Thirteen years ago, Joey died in a plane crash accident. The assistant manager took over. His name was Kevin Arnold. Now, Kevin was a bit younger and an upstanding Christian man."

"Was?" She didn't like where this seemed to be headed.

"Yeah. He noticed some discrepancies with the weight numbers of shipments. The irregularities spurred him to start asking questions. Someone told him to speak to me, which he did. We talked about what I suspected, and he figured I was right. He called some reporter at the New Orleans paper to help him uncover the truth. Two nights after that, someone murdered him in his own driveway."

Nausea burned her stomach. "His own driveway?"

"Kinda familiar, isn't it? Now you can see why I let the matter drop after I was attacked in my driveway."

"How's this tie to Senator Mouton?"

"Sheriff Thibodeaux investigated, if you could call it that. Within a few days, he closed the case. Unsolved." He rested his chin in his palms. "Next thing I hear, Roger's retired and is named manager at the rice plant, on Senator Mouton's personal recommendation."

"And you verified this?"

"Of course. Not only that, but the last act Roger Thibodeaux performed as sheriff was to hire his nephew Martin Gocheaux as deputy—the officer who worked my case. And from what I've learned since, the port hired on one of Roger's other nephews to work the night shift on the dock."

Mr. Lewis stood and gave her a penetrating stare. "You tell me, Ms. LeBlanc. It all sounds rather convenient, doesn't it?"

SEVENTEEN

"What are we looking for?" CoCo whispered.

Silence prevailed in the library, save for the occasional book falling, pages fluttering, or conversations murmuring. Alyssa sat before the microfiche machine, scrolling through the front section of the local paper for the week after her parents were killed.

Murdered.

"I don't know. Anything that strikes you as odd."

CoCo mumbled, turning her machine's knob, fast-forwarding to the next page. She had taken the parish paper while Alyssa ran through the tiny Lagniappe weekly edition. She should be grateful the library had a microfiche machine, even if it had been there since the Dark Ages.

Alyssa had spent the time waiting for CoCo to return from her morning run by writing up another interview with Mr. Lewis and sending the article to Simon. She wished she could include what she'd learned this morning, but couldn't betray her source's confidence. Even if she didn't yet know if she believed him or not.

How many articles could a small town have about a local talent show and a church bake sale?

Then a headline grabbed her attention.

Rice Plant Manager Shot in Chest.

Alyssa magnified the article and read. Her heart raced, pumping adrenaline into her veins.

Kevin Arnold, Manager at Gibson Rice Plant, was shot in the chest at his home Friday night. Sheriff Thibodeaux states the parish office believes the crime to have been committed by an outsider. No suspects identified at this time.

Big surprise. This coincided with what Lewis had told her. She maneuvered the screen to identify the date. She gasped, pinpricks of dread assaulting her conscience.

Kevin Arnold had been murdered the same night as her parents.

"What?" CoCo whispered and looked over Alyssa's shoulder.

Alyssa waited for her sister to finish reading.

"I don't get how this is important."

"Mr. Lewis told me that Mr. Arnold had been the plant manager before Roger Thibodeaux." Alyssa fought to organize all the data in her mind. "For him to be shot and killed the same night as the car crash... well, it just seems too much of a coincidence, don't you think?"

"Hmm. Maybe."

"Keep looking and see what you find out in your paper."

"All I've found is the article on the car accident that states you were rushed to the hospital."

"Does it tell if the sheriff launched an investigation?"

CoCo pursed her lips as she read. "No. Not that I can tell."

"See if there's an article about Mr. Arnold's murder."

Her sister nodded. "Yep, right here on the next page. Doesn't give much more information than what your paper stated." She leaned back in her chair, pinching the bridge of her nose. "I understand how it looks, but I'm not getting a connection."

"We have to dig deeper."

CoCo glanced at her watch. "I'm gonna have to dig later. I promised Luc and Felicia I'd help them plan the party. Somebody has to stand up to their mother."

"What party?"

"Felicia and Frank's engagement party, silly. It's this weekend. I hope you're planning on attending."

"Sure." Unless she'd returned home by then. Somehow, the idea of leaving Lagniappe didn't excite her as much as it would have last week. She didn't have her usual, overwhelming need to get away. And on this trip, she definitely had even more reason to hate the bayou and want to go home. Her about-face didn't make sense. Why wasn't she chomping at the bit to get outta here?

Because of the case? The story? Or, Jackson Devereaux?

She didn't want to analyze her emotions just yet. Not over him. Alyssa allowed her sister to help her out of the library to the Jeep. The swelling on her ankle had gone down, but soreness still throbbed occasionally. Meanwhile, her mind flipped through her mental filing cabinet of information. There had to be a link between Kevin Arnold's murder and her parents'—she just knew it. Now she had to uncover it.

CoCo dropped her off at home before heading to the Trahan house. Alyssa reviewed her notes again. Where was the connection? Frustration filled her after two hours.

She tossed her notes aside and wandered downstairs to check on her grandmother.

Grandmere stood at the stove, stirring a pot of gumbo. The tang of seafood hovered in the air, blending with the aroma of pepper and spices. How many times in her teen years had she come into the kitchen to find Grandmere cooking comforting meals? Never once understanding Alyssa's embarrassment over her family, Grandmere offered love and comfort the best way she knew. How often had Alyssa lashed out in anger over her situation— lashed out at the one person who always had a hug for her and love to offer? Could she recall a single time she'd told Grandmere she loved her? Aside from when Grandpere died? Remorse choked her.

What if she'd lost her grandmother this past week? Without letting her know what lurked under the surface in her heart? What had always been in her heart, even if her immature mind wouldn't allow her to recognize it, much less admit it? Love and gratitude burst through her. Alyssa wrapped her arms around her grandmother, hugging her from behind.

"My, *ma chère,* that's nice." Grandmere leaned back into the embrace.

"I love you, Grandmere." The words were so emotion-riddled that Alyssa barely managed to squeak them out.

"*Je t'aime,* too, child."

Tara chose that moment to explode into the kitchen, slamming the screen door in her wake. "Something smells marvelous." She bounded into the room, her youthfulness brightening the space. She grinned at Alyssa. "You aren't helping cook, are you?"

Alyssa crinkled her nose. "No, Ms. Smarty-pants."

"Whew, what a relief." Tara chuckled. "Grandmere, you need me to help you with anything?"

"*Non,* child. It's all set. Only has to simmer for a couple of hours."

"I'm gonna run out to the shed for a bit."

"Need my help?" Interest flashed into Grandmere's face.

Tara grinned. "I can always use your help, yes."

Cold seeped into Alyssa's bones as she lowered herself to a chair, easing the weight off her ankle. "You're going out there to do that voodoo stuff, aren't you?"

"Leave it alone," Tara snapped. Her eyes blazed with both annoyance and anger.

"But it's nonsense. Silly parlor-type games."

"Then why does it bother you so much, Al?"

"Because people think we're crazy." There, she'd said it. Finally, after trapping her pain in her heart for so many years, she'd let it out.

"Is that why you hate it here so, child?" Sadness glistened in Grandmere's eyes.

Tears burned Alyssa's eyes. "People think we're bonkers… odd and different."

"Oh, *ma chère,* of course we're different."

"I don't like being different."

Suddenly, she'd drifted back to high school.

"Alyssa LeBlanc makes straight A's because her grandmother puts hexes on her teachers," a bouncy cheerleader quipped.

"Too bad her grandma can't whip up a love potion so Alyssa can get a date." The head cheerleader, director of these girls who made Alyssa's life miserable, glared at her with contempt.

"Maybe she could get her big sister to do that. I hear she's learning from grandma," one of the other girls in the clique said.

"Yeah, I heard that, too." The head cheerleader smiled. *"What about you, Ally? Are you gonna cast a spell on me now?"*

Their laughter filled her head, her heart. She wanted the hall to close in and swallow her.

"What are you so afraid of, child?"

Alyssa snapped her attention to her grandmother, back to the present. "I just don't want to be laughed at anymore." Tears spilled from her eyes. She swiped them away, hating that anyone, even her family, bore witness to her weakness.

"Who laughed at you?" Tara's tone changed from one of accusing to concern.

"Nobody." Great, another traumatic memory to keep the ones from her past company. Joy and rapture.

"I'm going to put a protection ring around you," Tara said, her back stiff.

"No, don't even th—"

Her words fell on deaf ears as Tara stormed from the house. Alyssa stared at her grandmother. "Grandmere, I know this is what you do, but it's wrong. Can't you see that?"

"Oh, child, it's not just what I do. It's who I am." Her grandmother smiled and touched her cheek. "It'll be okay, *ma chère*. All is well."

Alyssa watched Grandmere follow Tara to the shed.

No, nothing was okay. Nothing could be considered well.

Least of all her emotional state.

Jackson staggered from the docks, down the gang-plank and to his truck. He'd gotten all the copies he could make in the office. Time was running out. The fake social security number would return any day now, and then the jig would be up. Jackson steered into the parking lot of the local diner. He sat in a booth in the back of the small eatery and ordered coffee. Alone, he pulled out the copies of the bills he'd made and studied them.

Every single one of them connected to a shipment from the rice plant. Registering the dates, he could almost verify they coincided with the days Bubba found the money in the bayou. In the bill of lading's account receivable notations, under the plant's address, were the initials R.T. The person at the plant who'd checked the shipment on the truck to send to the dock. Jackson flipped through the papers again. All of the bills had the initials R.T.

The waitress swooped by with his coffee and left. Jackson stared at the copies again.

Maybe this R.T. at the rice plant could shed some light on the matter.

R.T....

Roger Thibodeaux!

Why couldn't she sleep?

Maybe since she knew she drew closer to the truth, the knowledge caused her restlessness. Or could it be because Jackson Devereaux's image kept flitting into her mind? Alyssa tossed the comforter aside and padded to her laptop on the desk. No pain shot up from her ankle. She must have merely stressed it.

Could the time have come to tell him about her mother and that he'd taken the job she'd coveted? That she'd vowed five years ago to best him?

Her sister's voice drummed in her ears. *Take everything to God.*

Alyssa started to push the notion aside, but stopped. CoCo had such peace, seemed so content with life. Could her personal relationship with God have something to do with the tranquility?

Yearning rose up in her chest. She wanted that peace. Wanted that calmness and acceptance. Wanted to be loved for herself.

Alyssa lowered her head and closed her eyes, and prayed to the God of her sister.

EIGHTEEN

The morning sun streaked the sky, as if God's fingertip had brushed a stroke of violet across the blue masterpiece. Alyssa stared out the open window of her bedroom. Birds chirped, their song carried on the soft breeze floating over the bayou. Maybe Lagniappe wasn't the cursed place she'd always thought it to be.

She smiled at herself. This morning, she'd awoken with a prayer on her lips. Could being in a relationship with God be so easy? She'd even dug into her dresser drawers to find her old Bible, looking up passages about Jesus being her intercessor, comforter and defender. To feel comfortable just talking to Him...well, her heart soared.

Alyssa turned from the window. Her gaze fell on the photograph on her bedside table. Momee and Papa, just months before their deaths. They looked so happy, so in love, so at peace. Had God been a daily part of their lives? She wished she could ask. Alyssa traced her finger along the picture, over Momee's image. Her heart turned as cold and fragile as the glass.

Who did she think she was fooling? Alyssa would never ease her guilt of surviving by honoring her mother in journalism. Her therapist had explained survivor's guilt and all, but now, here in the bayou with a new sense of confidence, she had to ask herself the hard questions. Had she really always wanted to be a journalist, or had she been trying to gain her mother's approval? For so long she'd thought following in her mother's footsteps would be what she wanted most. But now? She honestly didn't know. She'd scrambled and fought to make a niche for herself in journalism, but she hadn't actually considered if this was truly her heart's desire. Could she have deluded herself for all these years, determined to follow in the wake of her mother's ghost?

For the first time, Alyssa took inventory of her thoughts and emotions. Did she really have passion to be a journalist? The answer numbed her.

While she enjoyed the fast-paced flow of the job, she didn't want to write within the confines of the facts. In truth, she felt drawn to something else. Oh, she still wanted to write. She'd always loved the written word. The idea of putting the stories in her mind onto paper beckoned to her. She just didn't want to be a reporter.

Should she chuck journalism to become a novelist? Someone plagued by rejections and reservations.

She set down the photograph, her mind filled with doubts.

Are you proud of me yet, Momee?

The slamming of the front door drew her from her musings.

"Al, you up?" CoCo hollered.

Alyssa smiled. If she hadn't been, her sister's bellow would have woken her. "Yep." She moved to the stairs, fully dressed.

"Wow, you're ready for the day. Come on, let's have breakfast. Grandmere's making pancakes."

The smell of warmed cane syrup hovered in the kitchen. Alyssa smiled as she took her seat, spying the can of syrup sitting in a pan of water on the stove.

"Good morning. Hot off the griddle." Grandmere flipped two cakes onto a plate, slapped a thick pat of butter on top before coating them in the warm syrup. She set the plate in front of Alyssa. The butter had already melted, oozing down the stack.

Alyssa waited for Grandmere to set CoCo's plate in front of her. "Would you pray, CoCo?"

Her sister's eyes widened, but she smiled and nodded. They bowed their heads, and CoCo offered up grace for the meal, along with asking for the health and protection of their family. When they lifted their heads, Alyssa thought she caught a glimmer of tears in CoCo's eyes. Her sister loved her. The thought warmed Alyssa more than the heated syrup.

"What're your plans for today?" CoCo asked.

"I was thinking of talking with Jackson and seeing if he could use his connection with the New Orleans paper to find out what Momee was working on when she... died." The word still sat sideways in her mouth. She took a drink of coffee.

"Do you think it's important?"

"Maybe." Alyssa shrugged. "It's something to look into. Then I'm going to try to get copies of the police reports on Kevin Arnold's murder. Surely there's something filed that's a matter of public record."

"I'll be happy to help you later this afternoon. After I finish my run this morning, I'm going over to Luc's to help Felicia pick out a dress for the party. But then I should be free."

"I don't know what time I'll get to meet with Jackson.

He's working on the docks at night, so he might sleep in."
And she didn't know if he'd be willing to help her once
she came clean. Her heart ached.

After CoCo left, Alyssa booted up her laptop and
logged onto the Vermilion parish clerk of court's Web site.
She maneuvered until she found the page with access to
public documents. Minutes fell off the clock as she
scrolled through the dates. Fortunately, the records had
all been computerized three years ago, allowing all the
old documents to be available. At last, she retrieved the
records from the month and year of the murder. She rolled
her mouse through page after page.

She didn't find a report on Kevin Arnold's murder, but
she did find one with her parents' names.

Stomach knotting, Alyssa clicked on the file.

She scanned the information. Her heart dropped to her
knees. The sheriff's office had conducted an investigation
into the accident. For two days.

Only two.

After which, they deemed the car crash an accident.
Driver's fault.

Alyssa's hands trembled.

She read until the end of the document. Only one line
stuck out at her—the name of the investigating officer.

Sheriff Roger Thibodeaux.

"I'm glad you called." Jackson stared across the table
at Alyssa. Her eyes were hooded, and the beginnings of
black circles formed under her eyes.

The clanking of silverware, people moving, and talk
from other diner patrons vanished as he studied her.

A haunted woman.

His heart tightened.

"I made a big connection last night," he offered.

Her eyes lit up. His heart responded with a backflip. Without stopping to consider his own reactions, he told her what he'd learned from the bills of ladings coinciding with the rice plant and shipment numbers.

Her face turned pale. He couldn't read her expression.

"What's wrong, Alyssa?"

"This is getting more frightening the further along we go." She proceeded to tell him that Roger Thibodeaux had been the sheriff who'd worked the cases of both her parents' car accident and the assault on Warren Lewis, along with sharing the allegations of Mr. Lewis.

He let the information sink in. "Do you believe Mr. Lewis is telling the truth?"

"Absolutely. At least, he believes he's telling the truth." She rubbed her scar. "His allegations about Senator Mouton don't ring true to me, though."

"Let me get this straight. Roger Thibodeaux was the sheriff when three seemingly unrelated crimes were committed, and he worked each of them. He's now the rice plant manager, apparently having landed the job on Senator Mouton's recommendation."

She nodded.

"And I've proven all the numbers found on money in the bayou matched the shipment numbers to rice plant shipments. All had his initials on the bills."

Definitely too much to be considered coincidence.

"How do your parents' deaths relate?"

She shifted in her chair. "The car accident that gave me my scar? Well, my parents died in the crash."

Now he understood her reaction to his probing questions. "I'm so sorry." How awful. No wonder she detested Lagniappe so much.

"Here's the thing, though. I occasionally have nightmares about the crash, but recently, I've had another memory resurface, and now I'm one hundred percent positive the wreck wasn't an accident. It was murder. Someone killed my parents."

And could have killed her. His stomach clenched.

She continued, obviously unaware of his gut reaction. "I know it's been a long time—thirteen years ago—but I know I'm right. They were murdered, and the crime written off as an accident. By Roger."

He shook his head. "It's so much to consider. And you feel like they're connected in some way?"

"I don't know, but I'm beginning to believe all of this is related."

"Me, too." He stared into his black coffee, his thoughts tumbling over each other.

"In my research at the library, I found out someone killed Kevin Arnold the same night my parents were murdered."

She certainly seemed convinced. Her belief was not only reflected in her words, but also in her face. "Something else interesting. Martin Gocheaux is Roger Thibodeaux's nephew. Roger got him hired on in the sheriff's office before he retired to work at the rice plant." Her eyes danced. "According to Mr. Lewis, another one of Roger's nephews works on the docks."

"Definitely too chancy to be considered a fluke, in my humble opinion." He studied her. Something akin to dread marred her beautiful features.

Beautiful? Had he really just thought that?

As he took in the sight of her, recalling her smile and

laugh, her gentleness and concern, he realized he *did* find her beautiful. Inside and out.

"Jackson, there's something I need to tell you."

He ran a finger around the rim of his mug. Whatever she had to say, it didn't look as if she wanted to tell him.

She sucked in a deep breath. "I haven't been exactly forthcoming with you."

"About?" A sinking feeling washed over him.

"Do you remember the day you got your promotion at the *Times-Picayune?*"

He searched his recollection. "Uh, vaguely."

"I interviewed for that job."

His mind raced through his memory files. His heart thudded hollowly.

Big dark eyes. Small girl, with long, dark hair.

Jackson stared at her. Different color and length of hair. But the same girl. No, now a woman.

"You."

She nodded.

So what? They'd both applied out for the same position. That wasn't anything to get all worked up about. Unless…

"You resent that." His muscles tensed. "You resent me."

"No. Yes. Ugh." She shook her head. "I did. At first. But not now."

So that's why she'd been so back and forth in the way she acted toward him. She didn't like him at all. And she'd planned on using him from the get-go! Why hadn't he seen her ploy sooner?

"Because you need me for this story, right?" Anger simmered under his skin. "A story that could make your career."

"No. I mean, I do need you, but that's not what I mean."

He chose to ignore the lines of frustration digging into her face. She used him to get a story. Paying him back for winning the job she'd applied for. Stringing him along.

She'd made him care for her. Caused him to think he could fall in love with her. Foolish.

"Jackson."

He glared into her eyes, not bothering to shield the disappointment and resentment. "What?"

"I realized something this morning."

"Am I supposed to be enthralled by a revelation of yours?"

The hurt in her eyes stung him.

Lord, help me to forgive her as You forgive me.

She leaped from the chair. "Not that it matters, but I realized this morning that I don't even want to be a reporter anymore." She turned and rushed from the diner.

Running away—wasn't that her modus operandi? The bayou, the newspaper, the sandwich shop and now?

Jackson tossed bills on the table and followed her. He caught her on the sidewalk, and grabbed her arm. "Wait, *chère.* I'm sorry."

"No, it's me who should be sorry. And I am." She lifted tear-filled eyes. "I really am sorry, Jacks."

Her use of his nickname did the trick.

He pulled her into his arms, and lowered his lips to hers. She tasted like coffee and sugar. He deepened the kiss. Her arms wrapped around his neck, her fingers threading into his hair. His heart found a new gear—warp speed.

Reluctantly, he ended the kiss, not trusting the emotional stirring in his chest.

Oh, he could get used to kissing Alyssa LeBlanc.

Very used to it, indeed.

NINETEEN

Alyssa stared into Jackson's eyes. Their kiss left her legs feeling as liquid as CoCo's gravy. She swayed for a moment, grateful his arms still held her. Strong, muscular arms.

She shook her head, clearing her mind. While still new at this whole personal-relationship-with-God thing, she knew the importance of keeping her thoughts pure. Very important. She let out a long breath of air. *God, tell me how to act the way You want me to.*

"I, uh, I'm—" His cheeks were an interesting shade of pink.

She pressed her finger against his lips. "Let's not analyze this right now. Okay?"

He nodded, and she dropped her hand. "I really am sorry for not telling you immediately, Jackson."

His expression remained soft. "Look, let's take a little walk around the square. Talk a bit. The fresh air will do us both good." He dropped his arms, but grasped one of her hands in his.

Well-built hands.

Stop it! Concentrate on putting one foot in front of the other.

Alyssa walked along the cracked sidewalk, glee and giddiness worrying against common sense and restraint inside her.

"What's this about you not wanting to be a reporter anymore?"

That threw cold water on her wandering thoughts.

"I did an inventory of my life this morning—where I am, what I want. I realized today I never should've become a reporter. I don't like it. I fooled myself into believing I wanted it."

"Why?"

"Because my mother was an award-winning photojournalist at the *Times-Picayune*." She teetered over a hole in the sidewalk, only to have Jackson grab hold of her elbow and steady her.

"And it was expected of you to follow in her footsteps?"

"No. I did that on my own. I guess because I wanted to honor her." *Or make her proud of me.*

"But she was a photographer. Did you ever think of doing that?"

She laughed. "I don't have the eye for it. Trust me, I tried."

"No wonder you were miffed I got the job. You wanted the position because it was where your mother worked."

"Silly, isn't it?" Concentration became even more difficult as he rubbed his thumb along the backside of her hand.

"Actually, it makes a lot of sense. And helps me understand you a lot better." He stopped and faced her. His movements were precise as he drew her into his arms and kissed her again.

She felt as if a feather tickled her stomach. Or a whole mass of butterflies had suddenly burst free inside her.

He pulled back, took her hand again and smiled.

His smile shook her nearly as much as his kisses.

"And in case you haven't noticed, I really like understanding you."

Alyssa giggled, the glee and giddiness winning the battle. "I like understanding you, too."

They continued around the square, the morning sun shining directly on them.

"So, if you don't want to be a reporter, what do you want to do?"

"I don't know." Heat spread across her face.

"Come on, you must have an idea. Where does your passion lie?"

"I think about stories a lot."

"Stories? You mean articles? That's reporting, *chère*." He chuckled.

"No, like fiction stories."

"As in a novelist?"

"Yeah. Stupid, huh?"

"Not at all. Half the reporters I know have the dream of taking time off to write the great American novel."

"I've got some ideas brewing around in my head."

"Maybe you should try putting them on your laptop."

She laughed. "Maybe I'll do just that."

A comfortable hesitation followed before he spoke again. "How's your grandmother?"

"Ornery as ever. Gotta love her." A smile tickled her lips. "How's the sheriff?"

"No official change."

She caught the hope in his voice. "But unofficially?"

"One of the nurses told me that Bubba moved his feet yesterday in response to stimuli."

"That's wonderful."

"Well, the doctors say the reaction was just that, a physical reaction. No thought required to perform."

"You think differently?"

"Yeah. I know God's in control of the situation, and I have to believe He'll bring it to closure for the best."

The burning question nearly seared her lips. "And if He doesn't?"

Jackson stopped and stared at her. "Huh?"

"If God doesn't heal the sheriff, how will you feel then?"

"I'll be sad, of course, and I wouldn't understand, but I know it'd be part of God's master plan."

Wow. Unbelievable. "You'd still be of the opinion God was in control?" Memories of the anger she'd felt when her parents died assaulted her.

"Of course. Alyssa, we may never understand why things happen the way they do, may never understand this side of Paradise, but one thing we can always cling to is that God's always in control."

"I wish I could grasp that. I'm still mad about Momee and Papa dying." Her heart clenched as more memories flooded.

"Here's the thing about faith. You come to the edge of a drop-off and you know one of two things will happen— either there will be a ledge to step on, or you'll sprout wings to fly."

She closed her eyes, barely able to concentrate as he stroked beneath her lip. "Jacks?"

"Yeah?" His voice was husky.

"Could you find out what my mother was working on for the paper at the time of her murder?"

He dropped his hands, clenching his fists to avoid touching her.

Once again, she'd duped him. Made him think she

cared with how she'd returned his kisses. Made him feel as if they were connecting on a spiritual level.

Then hit him with a plea for help.

One that required the use of his job. The job she'd wanted.

Could her manner all be an act? Even saying she didn't want to be a reporter? Man, she was good. Real good. Too good.

Alyssa blinked her eyes open. "What?"

"What's her name?" he ground out.

"Claire LeBlanc. Jackson, what's wrong?" She latched onto his arm.

"Nothing." He shrugged off her touch. He couldn't think clearly when she touched him. "Look, I have an errand I need to run. I'll find out what I can and let you know."

"Jacks?"

And he really couldn't think when she called him by his nickname.

"I'll call you." He forced himself not to sprint the final length to his truck.

Stupid, stupid, stupid. How could he have believed she'd really be interested in him? She'd played him, and he'd gone right along with it. Every step of the way.

Stupid.

He slammed the truck's door and peeled out of the parking lot. *Lord, I need some help, here.* He steered toward the hospital. He really needed to see Bubba, even if his friend couldn't give him any advice.

The nurse on duty smiled as he passed her. Bubba lay still, same as usual. The beeps and hums of the machines soothed Jackson's agitated nerves. He pulled up the chair and took his friend's hand.

"Pard, I sure wish you could talk to me. I'm all

messed up. Over a woman." He shook his head and stared at a cracked tile of the ICU. "I don't know how it happened, but I think I gave her my heart. And she stomped on it."

Bubba's hand shifted in his. Jackson loosened his grip. "Sorry, didn't mean to squeeze so tight. I'm just so frustrated. I've never felt like this before."

He took a deep breath, letting go of Bubba's hand. Jackson rested his elbows on the bed, cradling his head in his hands. "I think I'm falling in love with her, and I don't know how to stop it. I want to stop it. I think I do. I mean, she doesn't really care about me, so why would I want to love a woman like that?"

Bubba gripped his arm and squeezed.

"I know, I'm just having a pity party and I need to snap—" He jerked his stare to Bubba's face.

His friend blinked back at him.

"Bubba!" Jackson jumped to his feet, knocking over the chair, and pressed the call button over the bed. "Bubba, you're awake. Can you hear me?"

The sheriff blinked rapidly.

A nurse rushed into the room. "What's the mat—" She looked at Bubba. "Oh, my. I'll get the doctor." She hurried out.

"How do you feel?" Jackson grabbed his friend's hand again. "Blink if you're in pain."

Again, Bubba blinked.

"Don't worry about it. The nurse went to the get the doctor." He squeezed the sheriff's hand a little tighter. "Oh, praise God, Bubba. I've been praying so hard for your healing. God is so good."

A doctor whooshed into the room, the tails of his white coat flying behind. "Please step back," he said.

Jackson moved against the wall.

The doctor shined the light in Bubba's eyes. "Mr. Theriot, I'm Dr. Wahl. I'm just going to look you over right quick."

Once more Bubba blinked.

The doctor flitted over the sheriff, his hands moving. He spoke quickly and used words Jackson didn't understand as the nurse's pen flew over the chart.

"We're going to take some tests. Are you comfortable? Blink once for yes."

Bubba blinked. A definite response!

Jackson's heart pounded harder than when he'd kissed Alyssa.

Thank You, Father. Thank You for this miracle.

"Once we affirm you're to the next level, we'll remove the tube from your throat. We'll know more once the tests are concluded and we have the results. Do you understand?"

Bubba blinked once.

The doctor smiled, patted Bubba's shoulder and motioned Jackson into the hall. The nurse lifted the phone and ordered tests.

"I'll be right here, pard," Jackson said before following the doctor.

"This is quite amazing," the doctor said. "To be honest, I expected his organs to fail within the next seventy-two hours or so."

Hope rose in Jackson's gut. "But he's doing well, right?"

"He looks better than we could ever have expected. We'll run several tests and know more definitely then."

"But he's awake. That's the main thing."

"It's difficult to say, Mr. Devereaux. We'll need to see

if he has any brain damage or swelling on the brain. His organs took a major hit in the assault and were put on a machine to make them work. We can't be sure what lasting damage will remain until we get the test results back."

No, God remained in control of this. Just like Jackson had told Alyssa.

"I understand what you're telling me, Dr. Wahl, but I know he's gonna be just fine."

The doctor finally smiled. "How can you be so sure?"

"Because God's holding Bubba in the palm of His hands. He is, after all, the Great Physician, and He's still on the throne."

TWENTY

"You'll never believe it, Al." CoCo rushed into Alyssa's bedroom, her face flushed.

Alyssa set down the Bible. After Jackson had left her so abruptly, she'd had the strongest urge to read some Scripture. She'd changed into comfortable jeans and a T-shirt before diving into reading. "What?"

"The sheriff. He's come out of the coma!" Her sister danced across the floor. "Isn't it wonderful?"

Incredulity mixed with the desire to believe filled Alyssa. "When? How?"

"God's miracle. His healing touch. Our prayers have been answered."

"I don't understand."

"A nurse called Luc while I was at his house and told him. Said that Jackson had been visiting, talking to the sheriff, when suddenly he grabbed Jackson's arm."

"I don't know what to say. This is amazing. The doctors told Jackson they didn't have much hope, since he'd been in a coma for so long."

"I know. It's all God, Al. He's so amazing."

Alyssa pushed to her feet, hesitated, then dropped back into the desk's chair. "I'm at a loss as to what we should do."

"Praise God, that's what we do." CoCo laughed. "Luc rushed to the hospital. He said he'd call later and let me know the details."

She caught her sister's happiness, laughing. "This is great news. We'll know who assaulted him."

CoCo froze, the smile falling from her face. "Oh, my. I just thought of something."

"What?"

"What if his attackers find out he's out of a coma?"

The same thought had crossed Alyssa's mind, along with her suspicion of Martin Gocheaux's involvement in the crime. His own deputy. If the nurse called Luc, she'd surely called the police. Putting the sheriff in danger.

Alyssa jumped to her feet. "We've got to get to the hospital."

"Why?"

"We need to make sure they post an officer at the sheriff's door. Not anyone with the local department, but one of those FBI agents." Alyssa rushed down the stairs and grabbed her keys. "Deputy Gocheaux might be involved."

"Should we call the hospital?"

"Get in. We'll call from the cell."

Alyssa stepped on the accelerator, spinning out of the driveway. Gravel pinged against the back bumper. CoCo jabbed the numbers on her cell phone. She let out a growl. "It's busy." She pushed the Redial button, then slammed the phone into the console. "Still busy. Does Jackson have any proof yet?"

Why did her sister assume Jackson would be the one securing proof and not her? Alyssa pushed down her inferiority complex, refusing to lose focus. As she steered the Honda toward the hospital, she relayed all she and Jackson had figured out.

CoCo shook her head. "And that's not enough to take to the FBI?"

"Not yet. It's all falling together in our minds, but we can't make the physical connection."

"You know, Felicia's fiancé works on the dock. Maybe you could talk to him and see what he knows."

Alyssa whipped into the parking lot, her mind stuttering. Jackson had said the sheriff set him up with someone working on the dock already. Someone who vouched for Jackson. Someone the sheriff apparently trusted. Could Luc's future brother-in-law be the one?

They rushed into the hospital's main entrance, passed the nurses' station and slipped into the elevator. Alyssa jabbed the button for the fourth floor. "What I still can't connect is if they are moving drugs, why didn't the DEA unit with the dog find them?"

"That is odd. Maybe they aren't smuggling drugs at all."

The elevator door opened and they turned down the hall.

"What else could it be? That money dropped has to be payment for something." Alyssa marched past the ICU waiting room.

"I'm working on trying to figure that out. Unless it's a new street drug the DEA hasn't made public yet. Takes time to train their dogs to pick up the new substances."

A nurse stopped them.

"We're here to see Sheriff Theriot," Alyssa said.

"I'm sorry. He's having tests conducted. No one is allowed inside right now."

"Is there a guard outside his room?" Alyssa blurted out.

The nurse flashed a look of pure annoyance. "That's really of no concern to you."

"CoCo."

They turned to see Jackson and Luc striding down the hall toward them.

Alyssa's heartbeat hitched as the men drew closer. Her tongue suddenly felt as crisp as the garlic bread she'd burned.

Luc draped an arm over CoCo's shoulder. "He's awake and alert. They're running tests now. Isn't it a miracle right from God's finger?"

Jackson didn't speak, just pinned Alyssa to the spot with his stare.

The stare that probed deep into her spirit.

She dropped her gaze to the floor and studied her shoes. She slowly took in her attire. Faded jeans and a large shirt. For a moment, panic pounded. She looked like the hillbillies she despised. But then she realized she didn't care what she wore or how she appeared. Right here, right now, none of that mattered.

"Did he say anything?" CoCo asked.

Jackson shook his head. "The tube's still in his throat. They'll take it out for the tests."

"Maybe he'll be able to tell us who did this," Luc said.

"Is anyone here from law enforcement?" Alyssa asked softly.

Luc nodded. "Deputy Anderson and one of the FBI agents are in the cafeteria getting coffee. The doctor told them it'd be about an hour or so before they were done running the tests on Bubba."

"Will he be put in a regular room?" Alyssa couldn't stand Jackson's staring. She shifted to face Luc and CoCo.

"Far as I know. Why?" Luc lowered his arm to her sister's waist.

"Because we have reason to believe someone in the sheriff's office was involved in the attack on Bubba," Jackson said quietly, still staring at her.

What was up with him? She'd apologized, and he seemed to have accepted. Then, as if he'd suddenly been doused in printer's ink, he'd rushed off to run an errand. Ran away from her. A splinter of hurt jabbed her heart. She shoved the feeling aside. Why did she care so much?

Because her heart had already become involved with Jackson Devereaux.

She gave herself a mental shake to concentrate on the conversation. Jackson and CoCo brought Luc up to speed on what they'd uncovered.

"So you think Martin was involved?"

"I do," Alyssa said.

"Have you shared this information with the FBI agents?"

Jackson shook his head. "They should have run a background check on every person connected to Bubba. If they had, they would know about Martin Gocheaux."

"But what if they didn't?" Luc asked. "Shouldn't you at least tell them? Isn't it irresponsible if you don't?"

"The thing is, my friend who gave me the information is in the FBI. They aren't supposed to share information with anyone outside the agency."

"Ah. I see." Luc ran a hand over his face. "So, what can we do?"

"Let me try to talk to Agent Lockwood." Alyssa surprised herself with her suggestion. "I think I might be able to convince him there's a threat without breaking any confidentiality." She didn't like either of the agents, thought they'd done a poor job of investigating, but she didn't want to put Jackson in an awkward position.

"What will you say?" CoCo asked.

"I'll think of something." Alyssa smiled. "They're in the cafeteria?"

Luc nodded. Alyssa strode toward the elevators, her mind racing. What would she say? She stepped inside the car. Just as the doors slid shut, a hand pushed them back. Jackson stepped into the elevator with her.

He made the tiny space seem even smaller. She inhaled, drawing in the fresh and spicy hint of his cologne. Her heart twisted into a knot.

"I thought maybe you'd like a little support."

She did. But could she appeal to the agent with Jackson close by? He already had her all tied up in knots. "Thanks, but I think I should probably do this myself."

Another one of those unreadable expressions carved into his face. "Then I'll just ride back up." The muscle in his jaw twitched.

"Jackson, I don't know—"

The doors slid open.

"Forget about it, Alyssa."

She stepped into the hall and faced him. "I don't know what's wrong between us. I—"

"Just go do what you need to do."

The doors closed before she could argue. Her heart sinking into her stomach, Alyssa headed to the cafeteria. Spotting the two lawmen wasn't difficult. Deputy Anderson wore his uniform, and Agent Lockwood had on a black suit. Big surprise. She approached them with small steps.

"Ms. LeBlanc." Deputy Anderson stood, color rising to his face. "Have you come to check on the sheriff?"

"Yes." She flashed him a smile. "I actually need to speak to the agent here in private for a minute, though."

Confusion clouded the deputy's face. "Oh. Okay." He grabbed his foam cup. "I'll just head back up."

"May I sit?" Alyssa asked when Anderson had left.

Agent Lockwood waved his hand over the seat. "What can I help you with, Ms. LeBlanc?"

She crossed her ankles under the metal table. "I've been doing some investigating in this situation."

"Have you, now?"

Alyssa ignored the sarcasm. "Yes. I've discovered some things I think might be of interest to you."

"Please enlighten me."

Okay, now his sarcasm just out-and-out annoyed her. She cleared her throat. "Deputy Martin Gocheaux has been implicated in crimes before. Never charged, of course, but it's on his record."

That got the stiff-neck's attention. "How do you know this?"

"I can't reveal my sources. But if you run a background check on him, you'll see what I mean."

"What's that got to do with the sheriff?"

Here's where the situation got sticky. "Well, I believe it's possible that Deputy Gocheaux's involved in the attack on Sheriff Theriot."

"What?" Agent Lockwood laughed. Literally threw his head back and gave a belly laugh. "Why would you even think such a thing?"

She gritted her teeth. "Did you know Martin Gocheaux is the nephew of former sheriff Roger Thibodeaux?"

"So? Lots of families have members going into the same profession. It's not uncommon."

"Are you aware of the accusations and unexplained co-incidences revolving around Thibodeaux?"

"Hearsay."

He truly set out to grate her nerves. "What about the missing money from the sheriff's evidence room?"

"How did you know about that?"

Ah, now she had him. "Sources." She leaned her forearms on the table. "Don't you find it odd that evidence—money, at that—comes up missing from the locked sheriff's office? Unless, of course, a certain deputy removed the money."

Anger flashed in his eyes. Good. About time he got emotional over this case.

"I don't know who's leaking information to you, but you're interfering in a federal investigation."

Now she laughed. "Interfering? Tsk, tsk, Agent Lockwood. Seems I know more about your case than you do. Could it be you aren't exactly doing your job?"

His face turned an interesting shade of red.

"Look, I don't want to get into a testosterone contest with you. All I'm asking you to do is to dig deeper into the deputy. Check out his connections and contacts." Alyssa took in a deep breath. "And post an agent at the sheriff's door. Not one of his own deputies."

The lines around his eyes had hardened with his tone.

"Please, Agent Lockwood."

His expression softened. "I'll post an agent at his door."

"Thank you." She stood, her knees nearly knocking together. How she crossed the cafeteria floor and slipped into the elevator without falling on her face was a mystery to her. As she pressed the button for the fourth floor, she mentally celebrated her victory. The door whooshed open and Jackson stood back against the wall, arms crossed over his chest.

The elation joined her heart in her toes.

Did she have to look so vulnerable?

Jackson pushed off the wall and moved in step with Alyssa. "So? How'd it go?"

"He'll assign an agent to guard the sheriff's door." Her gaze darted along the hall.

"What else?"

"He made no other promises. I thought that would be enough."

Why couldn't he just ignore the way she seemed to wiggle into his heart? Every time he looked at her, pain sliced through him like a knife. A slow, dull knife.

"Where's my sister?"

"She and Luc went to talk to the doctors. To see if there's any new information about Bubba's condition."

"Oh." She opened her mouth, then clamped her lips shut, as if she reconsidered saying anything more.

"While you were gone, I did what you asked."

"Which was what?" she questioned.

"I put in a call to one of the old-timers at the paper to see if he could dig up what your mom had been working on before…before the accident."

"Before she was murdered." Her voice quivered on the last word.

Jackson's heart pounded. He didn't want to be at odds with her. Not when he had a sneaking suspicion he'd fallen for her. "He said he'd get back with me tomorrow."

"Thanks."

No longer able to resist the echoes of his heart, he took

her elbow and drew her to him. "Alyssa, I need to know something."

"What?" Her breath fanned his face.

"Are you just using me, or do you care about me?"

Her eyes widened, the green flashing. "Do you really think that—that I'm just using you?"

He swallowed, his Adam's apple scraping against his throat. "I don't know. I just want to make sure because I think I'm fall—"

"Jackson, Alyssa, come here. The doctor has something to tell us about Bubba," Luc yelled.

TWENTY-ONE

"His trachea sustained damage in the assault. His vocal cords suffered the brunt of the injury. We don't know the full extent yet, but for now, he can't talk."

Alyssa held Jackson's hand tighter, trying to convey the support she offered him. He squeezed back. "But he's okay, right?"

Dr. Wahl gave a noncommittal shrug. "We can't say just yet. His organs are functioning. We were able to remove the breathing and feeding tubes without incident. The preliminary tests reflect a positive prognosis. But until we get the rest of the results back, I can't estimate the level of his recovery."

Agent Lockwood and Deputy Anderson exchanged glances in the semicircle. Law enforcement personnel and local townspeople filled the ICU waiting room. News of the sheriff's awakening had spread across the bayou.

"Can he communicate in any method? Writing or blinking?" Agent Lockwood asked.

"Both of his hands are incapacitated at this time. But his eyes are responsive."

"Maybe I could get him to blink answers?"

The doctor held up his hand. "Right now, Sheriff

Theriot needs his rest to recuperate. His body is drained and the tests have been exhaustive. No one will be allowed to see him for several hours. I'd suggest you all go home and come back later. We'll know more then."

Agent Lockwood pulled Agent Ward to the side. They conversed in whispers in the corner. Alyssa studied them. She'd love to be a fly on the wall.

"I guess there's no point in hanging around," CoCo said.

People filed from the waiting room until only a few remained.

"I need to let Felicia know what's going on. She'll be praying until I get back." Luc smiled as he mentioned his sister. He hugged CoCo to his side. "Wanna ride home?"

CoCo stared at Alyssa. "You leaving?"

Alyssa glanced at Jackson. "I'll be home shortly."

Her sister darted glances from Alyssa to Jackson. "Okay. Well then, I'll see you at home. I'll check on Grandmere and Tara."

Agent Lockwood nodded to Alyssa before moving to stand outside the sheriff's hospital room. Relief filled her. At least he kept his promise.

Jackson let go of her hand. Her heartbeat echoed in her ears. What had he been about to say before Luc interrupted them? Would he tell her now?

"I'm going to talk to the nurse for a second. She's let me see Bubba after visiting hours every day this week. Maybe she'll at least let me slip in and say goodbye."

Disappointment flooded her as he walked away. She'd really hoped to get the topic back to what Jackson had started before. She needed to make him understand she wasn't using him. Maybe she'd be brave enough to tell him just how much she really cared. Too much to turn back now.

Alyssa clasped her hands in front of her. Jackson moved from the nurses' station. He'd understand. But he didn't approach her. He slipped inside the sheriff's room.

The room felt colder than Jackson remembered. He stood over Bubba's bed, staring down at his friend. At least with all the tubes removed from his mouth, he looked more like the buddy Jackson loved.

Bubba opened his eyes. His lips curled into a smile of sorts.

"Didn't mean to wake you. Just wanted to check on you before I headed out."

Blink.

Deliberate. Now his friend stared intently at him.

"Are you trying to tell me something, pard?"

Blink.

Jackson pulled the chair next to the bed and sat. "One blink means yes?"

Again, a deliberate blink.

"All right. Two blinks means no, okay?"

Bubba blinked once.

"Do you know who did this to you?"

One blink.

Jackson leaned forward, his toe tapped the floor. "Was Martin Gocheaux involved?"

A fast blink.

It was one thing to suspect, but another to get confirmation. Both of Jackson's feet bounced against the floor. "What about Roger Thibodeaux—was he involved?"

Blink.

"Anybody else?"

Another blink.

"Someone else in the department?"

Nothing.

"Do you know the other man?"

One blink.

"Do I?"

Blink. Blink.

"Look, I've been working with Alyssa LeBlanc in unraveling all this. She's got me all tied up, but that's another story. Would she know this other man?" And if she did, why hadn't she recognized his voice?

No response.

"You don't know that either." Leaning back against the chair, Jackson flipped things over in his mind. "Is it someone from Lagniappe?"

A slow blink.

"And he's connected to Roger Thibodeaux and Martin Gocheaux?"

Another affirmative reply.

"I'm still working undercover on the docks. I found…"

Bubba blinked several times over.

"I'm on the right track with the docks, aren't I? The money in the bayou is payment for smuggling, isn't it? From the rice plant."

Another yes.

"Drug smuggling."

Two blinks.

Jackson cocked his head. "Not drugs? Are you sure?" He'd been so certain. "But it is smuggling, right?"

Bubba blinked.

Smuggling something other than drugs. What? Something worth a lot of money, obviously. Jackson flipped

through his past assignments. Drugs, illegal aliens—
which wouldn't apply here...

A recent article he'd written flared in his mind. Jackson
jumped to his feet. "Are they smuggling illeg—"

"You aren't supposed to be in here," Dr. Wahl admonished. "My patient needs his rest. You need to leave."

"Just a second, Doctor." Jackson turned back to Bubba.
"Illegal weapons?"

"You'll have to leave now, Mr. Devereaux."

"But—"

"Now."

Dejection headlined his emotions. He opened the door
and cast a glance over his shoulder to his friend.

Blink.

TWENTY-TWO

Jackson came out of the sheriff's hospital room, his face aglow.

The FBI agent huffed. "No one was supposed to be in there."

"Bubba communicated with me." Jackson faced Agent Lockwood. "He confirmed that Martin Gocheaux was one of his attackers. He confirmed Roger Thibodeaux was involved. He con—"

"How did he confirm anything?" the agent asked.

"I did what you said, got Bubba to blink a response. One blink for yes and two for no."

Agent Lockwood pulled out his notebook and scribbled. "Gocheaux and Thibodeaux involved. What else?"

"Someone else was, too, but I don't know that person."

"Anything else?"

"They're smuggling out of the rice plant, like Alyssa and I suspected, but it's not drugs."

"Then what?" Alyssa interjected.

He smiled at her. "Guns."

"That's why the DEA dog couldn't sniff out anything." Alyssa couldn't fight her smile.

"Bingo." Finally, they were getting answers.

"Excuse me," Agent Lockwood interrupted. "Guns are being smuggled out of the rice plant?"

Jackson nodded and explained about the rice plant and the intercoastal port.

"Haven't you two just been the busy little beavers?" Agent Lockwood asked when Jackson had finished.

"He's my friend and called me to help."

"Is there anything else you need to tell me?"

Alyssa wet her lips. "There have been allegations that Senator Mouton could be involved."

The agent rolled his eyes. "And the hits just keep on coming."

"Nothing proven. I haven't been able to link anything yet."

"And you won't, either. As of now, I'm going to order you two to stay out of my investigation. I'll call in ATF to investigate the gun-smuggling theory, but you two are to stay out of this. Got that?"

Neither Alyssa nor Jackson moved.

"If you don't, I'll have you arrested for obstruction of justice. I'm not kidding." Agent Lockwood threw them a final glare before yanking out his cell again.

Jackson grabbed her hand and headed to the elevators.

"The sheriff's okay?"

"He looks good. From the way he acted, there's nothing seriously wrong with his mind. He was totally coherent, knew what I was asking. Always the cop."

The elevator dinged. They stepped inside and Jackson continued. "I asked Bubba if you would know who the other men involved were, and he indicated he didn't know."

"I wish *I* did."

"I know."

The doors slid open. Alyssa led the way to the parking lot. She unlocked the Honda. "What are you going to do?"

"Follow you home, of course."

Goosebumps of joy raced up her arm. "Okay."

Remembering to keep her speed under the limit, Alyssa kept checking in her rearview mirror. Jackson's truck stayed on her tail. That could be a good thing.

Or bad.

Couldn't the woman drive any faster?

She was going as slowly as if she were out on a Sunday afternoon drive. Jackson tapped his fingers on the steering wheel and offered up thanksgiving for Bubba's healing.

The ringing of his BlackBerry interrupted his prayer.

"Jackson Devereaux."

"Hey, there. It's Mac."

"How're things back in the room?" The old news-hound had bestowed the nickname on the newsroom two decades ago, and everyone still used the moniker.

"Good. Listen, I went back and pulled everything we had on what Claire LeBlanc was working on at the time of her death. You have no idea how dusty it is in the storage room. You owe me."

"You got it. What'd you find?"

"There's nothing official here, but I did find her handwritten notes from her desk calendar. They were stuffed in a box marked her articles. Can you believe they kept all this?"

"Mac," Jackson ground out.

"Right. Well, according to her notes, she was following up on an old interview with the mayor of N'Orleans and also planned to head to her hometown to work on something undercover."

Jackson's heart leaped into his mouth. "Are there any notes on the undercover assignment?"

"Looks like she'd jotted down random phrases. None of it makes sense to me."

"What are the phrases?"

"Rice plant, then the name Kevin Arnold under that." Rustling of papers sounded over Mac's hoarse breathing, indicative of his many years smoking. "The name Roger is on the next page with a circle around it."

Bull's-eye.

Mac coughed. "There's a little rectangle on the side with the name Edmond in it. Has a question mark beside his name."

Oh, no. Lewis might be right.

"That's it. Any of this helpful?"

"All of it. Thanks, Mac. Can you fax it to me, here? I owe you one."

"You owe me more than that, boy." Mac harked out a wheeze before asking for the fax number.

Jackson tossed the BlackBerry into the truck's console and followed Alyssa into her driveway.

How would he find the words to tell her that she'd been right?

Her parents had been murdered.

She waited for him on the veranda. He dragged his feet as he trudged up the stairs. When he finally met her gaze, a sense of foreboding clawed its way into her chest.

"What?"

"I got a call on the way over."

"The sheriff?" Her heart thudded.

"No." Jackson nodded to the big rockers. "Sit down. I have something to tell you."

She dropped into a chair. "What?"

"I heard back from my man at the paper."

Oh, no. Her mother.

Alyssa dove her hand into her pocket for her lip balm. "What'd you find out?"

He ran a hand over his hair.

"Just say it."

He twisted his hands. "You were right. Your mother was working on something involving all this. Her hand-written notes are jumbled, but basically she wrote the words: rice plant, Kevin Arnold, Roger and Edmond. The notes are being faxed to Bubba's house."

She swallowed. Why hadn't she made the connection sooner? Lewis had told her Kevin Arnold had contacted a reporter at the *Times-Picayune* to help him expose the discrepancies at the rice plant. Of course, he'd contacted her mother. She hadn't picked up on the reference because her mother'd been a photojournalist, but to a layman, journalist and photojournalist were close enough. Hadn't Senator Mouton made the same implication?

Senator Mouton. Her mother had implied his involvement with his name in her notes. But how? Why? He'd helped build her mother's career. He spoke at her funeral. Surely he couldn't be involved. Dismay nearly choked her.

"Are you okay?" Jackson's gentle touch on her hand softened the heartache.

"She *was* murdered."

"We don't know that, but it looks like a definite possibility." His hand grasped hers.

"So this Kevin Arnold called her and asked for help." She closed her eyes, drawing strength from Jackson's touch. "Knowing Momee, she'd agree to help. She probably made some connections like we did—Roger Thibodeaux to the rice plant."

"*Chère,* you can let this drop if it's too painful."

She jerked her gaze to his face. Such concern and…what other emotion shone so brightly in his face? She shook her head. "No, I need to know. I have to know the truth."

"I understand."

"I need to figure out the link between the Senator and this smuggling." She stood, immediately missing the warmth of his touch as she did. "I still find it hard to believe he would be involved with anything that hurt my mother."

"I hope he wasn't." Jackson stood and laid a hand on her shoulder.

"But I have to know."

His gaze drifted from her eyes to her lips.

Her scar tingled.

As if he knew, he cupped her face in his hands. His thumb gently caressed her scar. She closed her eyes.

"I'm going to kiss you again, *chère.*" His voice came out husky, but she didn't have time to think about that before his lips were on hers. Moving softly, caressing her. She wound her arms around his neck, responding.

He ended the kiss well before she would have liked. He planted light feathery pecks against her cheeks, eyes and forehead before kissing her scar. She stared into his eyes.

"Now's not the time to have the discussion I wanted to, so I'll save it for later." He planted a final kiss on the end of her nose. "But we *will* eventually talk about this thing between us."

Alyssa watched him get into his truck and pull away. Her heartbeat raced as if she'd just been chased through the bayou.

Inside, CoCo sat on the couch beside Grandmere and Tara. She glanced up as Alyssa shut the front door. "Did you hear anything more about the sheriff's condition?"

She brought them up to speed on the sheriff's communicating with Jackson.

"So you were right?"

"Not only about that." She glanced at her grandmother, taking notice of her skin tone. Rosy, not the pallor she'd exhibited in the hospital.

"What else, *ma chère?*"

"Someone did set out to murder Momee." The tears she'd held back when Jackson had revealed what he learned sprang forth and made tracks down her cheeks.

"What are you talking about?" Tara asked.

Between sniffles, she filled her baby sister in on her memory and what she suspected. Then she told them about Momee's handwritten notes. "That's why they killed Momee and Papa."

"You don't know that for sure, Al," CoCo said.

"It sounds pretty definite to me." Tara jumped to her feet. "Why didn't anyone tell me about your dream?"

"I'm sorry. I should have. It's just been so…hectic."

"I can't believe you didn't say anything. You found the time to tell CoCo. Just because I'm the youngest doesn't mean you sh—"

"Enough, child." Grandmere shifted on the old floral couch. "Do you believe Senator Mouton could really be involved in something that would have harmed Claire?"

"Of course, he couldn't," CoCo interrupted. "He was her friend. Remember the lovely things he said at the funeral?"

"Aside from that." Grandmere peered into Alyssa's face. "You do think it's possible, don't you, *ma chère?*"

"I hope I'm wrong, but I do." Alyssa twisted her hands in her lap.

"How do we find out?" Tara asked.

"We can't. We don't. We leave it in the hands of the police." CoCo glanced at Alyssa. "The FBI and now the ATF are involved. We let them handle it."

"Like you let the police handle the investigation into Beau Trahan's death?" Tara spat out.

"Well, we certainly can't just go up to the senator and accuse him," CoCo retorted.

Alyssa felt all the blood drain from her face, leaving her chilled.

"Child, what's wrong?" Grandmere laid her hand over Alyssa's.

"That's it." Alyssa shoved to her feet so fast, her equilibrium faltered and dizziness washed over her.

"What're you talking about?" Tara asked.

"That's what Momee would've done. If she thought her friend, someone she cared about, could be involved in something like this, she would have confronted him."

CoCo's eyes widened. "She wouldn't have confronted the senator."

"*Mai, ma chère,* I think Alyssa may be right. Claire probably would have."

"And once the senator knew she was hot on his trail, he what? Denied it?" CoCo planted her hands on her hips.

"Or ordered her to be taken care of," Alyssa whispered. "Told someone to murder her and make it look like an accident."

TWENTY-THREE

"We've taken Martin Gocheaux into custody since Sheriff Theriot confirmed his involvement in the assault to me. We've also detained Roger Thibodeaux." Agent Lockwood glanced at his notes on the table before looking back at Jackson. "This is Garrett Olson from ATF."

The young man shook Jackson's hand. Jackson's head swam with information overload. Five days had passed since Bubba had come out of a coma. Five short days in which the government officials had followed up on Jackson and Alyssa's investigation like lightning.

"We're still working on getting the name of the other assailant from Roger and Martin, but so far, they aren't giving anybody up," said Agent Lockwood.

"But you'll keep trying?"

"Certainly." Olson grinned. Something told Jackson the ATF would like a crack at the old politician.

"Any luck on finding out details about Claire LeBlanc's accident?"

Lockwood nodded. "We're looking into it. I think Roger will break down and spill his guts once we get him to crack."

"With the information we've processed so far, we

believe Gocheaux was the man who chased Ms. LeBlanc in the bayou."

"And shot at her," Jackson reminded them. The memory gave him chills. "What about the dock manager, Burl?" Did the man know Jackson had been instrumental in implicating him?

"He claims Roger paid him not to inspect certain shipments. Says he had no clue what was in the crates," the FBI agent answered.

"We'll keep looking into his story. Right now," Olson popped his knuckles, "we're checking each and every connection to Roger and Martin. A couple of names have come up on both lists, so we'll start looking at them. Starting with the pilot they both apparently know."

"Ah, the money drops in the bayou."

Olson nodded. "Right. We figure if we get him, he'll tell us who else was involved, even if Roger and Martin never sing."

"Sounds like this is all wrapping up." Jackson made a final memo in his notebook and closed it. "And the senator?"

"We've tried to reach him for questioning, but his wife says he's out of town the rest of the week." Olson heaved to his feet. "We'll stay on it until we get the truth, Mr. Devereaux. And that includes the senator's involvement."

"Looks like we'll be done by the end of the month." Lockwood stood.

"Heard the sheriff will be just fine," Olson said.

Jackson smiled. "They moved him to a regular room yesterday. He'll start his physical therapy in a couple of weeks, but he should be able to come home before then."

"That's really good." Lockwood slapped his thigh.

"Well, just wanted to come by and give you an update. Felt like we kind of owed you an exclusive."

Kind of? Yeah, right. But Jackson kept his mouth closed and shook the agents' hands. "I appreciate it. Anything else I can do to help, let me know."

"Oh, one more thing," Lockwood said. "Will you tell Ms. LeBlanc we appreciate her assistance, too?"

Alyssa hung up the phone and stared at the picture of her parents. The call had been one of the hardest she'd ever made, but peace now flooded her. Right or wrong, she'd made her decision and there'd be no turning back.

I'm sorry, Momee, but I have to listen to my heart now.

She smoothed her white shirt before squeezing into the bathroom.

"You look pretty," CoCo told her. "You do, too, Tara."

The three sisters crowded into the bathroom, each putting final touches on their hair or makeup.

"Is Felicia over-the-moon excited?" Tara coated her lips with a mocha shade lipstick.

"She is." CoCo sprayed perfume on her wrist and rubbed. "They set Thanksgiving Day as the wedding date."

"Aw, how romantic." Tara sighed.

"I think it is." CoCo stepped into the hallway. "Come on, we're going to be late. Luc and Fels will kill me if I'm not there on time. Somebody has to run interference with Hattie."

"How is the mother of the bride-to-be?" Alyssa asked.

"Driving Fels crazy, of course." CoCo giggled and clapped her hands. "Come on, we need to get."

"I still have to finish my hair," Tara complained.

Alyssa laughed. Their cutting up while getting ready

for a big to-do brought back so many memories. Picking on each other and their taste in dresses before proms and homecomings. Dates waiting in the living room, having to listen to Grandmere and voodoo. A knot wedged in Alyssa's stomach. No, she wouldn't let bad memories spoil her happiness with her sisters. Not tonight.

"Come on," CoCo coaxed.

"Why don't you go on? Tara and I will be along shortly."

"Are you sure?" CoCo popped her hands on her hips.

Alyssa and Tara burst out laughing.

"What?" their oldest sister asked.

"You always did that." Alyssa waved toward CoCo. "Putting those hands on your hips and giving us orders."

"I did not."

"Yes, you did," Tara quipped. "Still do, apparently."

"Oh, you two." CoCo stuck her tongue out at them. "You'd better be right behind me."

Alyssa and Tara laughed while she strode away.

"You know, I understand why you cut and highlighted your hair."

Alyssa stared at her little sister in the mirror. "You do?"

"Yep." Tara blotted her lips on a tissue. "I've always lived in CoCo's shadow, too."

"That's not exactly it."

"Then explain it to me."

With her hip cocked, digging into the side of the counter, Tara had no idea how much she looked like CoCo. Alyssa bet she wouldn't appreciate the comparison.

"Al?"

"I wanted to change when I left Lagniappe. Be somebody different. Totally make myself over."

"Because you hate this place so much."

"Yes. No." Alyssa shook her head. She wasn't doing this right. "I did."

"And now?"

Alyssa shrugged. "I don't hate it so much."

Tara smiled. She really was a beautiful young woman. "Does that have anything to do with Jackson Devereaux being here?"

Heat washed over her face. "He's from New Orleans. Not Lagniappe."

"But he's here now."

Her little sister had a point. "Yes, he is."

"What do you plan to do about that?"

"What?"

Tara sighed and shook her head. "You know, you and CoCo are the big sisters—you're supposed to have a clue about what's going on. But neither one of you can figure out what's right in front of your faces."

"Well, please don't keep me in suspense. Tell me what I'm not seeing." This was fun, connecting with her sister.

"You're in love with him."

That wiped the smile off Alyssa's face. She grabbed the comb and picked at her bangs. "I can't be in love with someone I've only known for weeks." But she had a strong hunch her sister was dead-on right.

"Really?" Tara laughed. "Who do you think you're fooling?"

She set the comb on the counter. "Is it that obvious?"

Tara laughed again. "Only to those of us who know you." She wrapped an arm around Alyssa's shoulders. "Have you told him?"

"Mercy, no. I couldn't do that."

"Why not?"

"I just couldn't."

Tara made a clucking sound.

"What?"

"Well, it shouldn't be that big of a deal."

"How's that?"

Tara shrugged. "He's in love with you, too."

He knew the moment she walked into the Trahan house. He sensed her presence as he had that day in church.

Alyssa's smile lit up the foyer as Luc took her purse and directed her to the dining room for refreshments. Jackson noticed the other men in the room focusing on her as well. Something burned in his gut. He made quick strides to reach her. "Hi, there."

She looked at him, a laugh teasing her lips. The lips he wanted to kiss so badly he ached. "Hi, yourself."

"You look lovely." What an understatement. In black slacks and a white tuxedo-style shirt that accented every curve, she wasn't lovely. More like breathtaking.

"You clean up nice, too."

If he kept this up, he'd be drooling at her feet any second. "Let me get you a drink?"

"A cola would be nice. Thank you." Why did she seem so shy all of a sudden?

He headed to the set-up bar, grabbed a soft drink and returned to her. "Here ya go, *chère.*"

"Thanks." She took a sip, her eyes touching his soul over the rim.

"Agent Lockwood and the agent from ATF came by this afternoon."

"Really?"

He gave her a brief update. Brief because his tongue

felt as if it had swollen to three times its natural size, and words were hard to form.

"At least they're making progress. I just know in my heart now that Mouton is involved." She lowered her eyes. "And was involved with my parents' murders."

"They gave me all the information so I could write an article for the paper." He swallowed. Hard. "I made you a copy of my notes for your piece."

"I'm not going to write a piece on this."

"You aren't?" Didn't she realize he'd handed her what would probably the biggest story of her career so far? "Why not?"

"I quit my job today."

"You really did it?"

Alyssa laughed, that throaty sound that did strange things to his insides. "Now you sound like my editor Simon."

"Are you sure about this?"

"I don't want to do it anymore. And besides, I don't want to compete with you."

He took a moment to study her, really look into her eyes. She had a serenity about her. "Are you going to put your stories on your laptop now?"

She smiled. "I'm going to try."

"That's great, *chère*. You'll be awesome."

"At least I have some money saved up to live on. And CoCo told me I could move back home."

"Sounds like you've got it all worked out."

"For a while, anyway."

"Why, Alyssa LeBlanc, how wonderful to see you," a woman said in a high-pitched tone. Loudly.

Alyssa winked at Jackson. "Luc's mother," she mouthed at him before turning to face Hattie Trahan.

"Mrs. Trahan, how lovely to see you. And don't you look smashing."

Hattie patted her pristine hair. "Aren't you precious to say such a thing?" Her gaze lit on Jackson. "I don't believe I've had the pleasure. I'm Hattie Trahan."

Oh, he'd known many of these older debutantes back in New Orleans. He bowed low and kissed her proffered hand. "Jackson Devereaux."

"My, if I were younger, I do believe I'd swoon."

A blush hinted on Alyssa's face. He wanted to laugh, but knew she'd probably belt him one if he did. "It's an honor to meet you, Mrs. Trahan."

Luc appeared at her side. "Mother, can I steal you away for a minute? The caterers have questions."

Hattie waved her hand at Jackson and Alyssa. "A woman's work is never done. I'll see y'all later."

Jackson had never felt such gratitude before as when Luc whisked Hattie away. "She's quite the character I take it?"

Alyssa opened her mouth to reply, then froze. All peace fled her face. She turned whiter than white.

"What is it?" He grabbed for her elbow.

"Him," she whispered.

"Who?"

"Senator Mouton. He's here."

TWENTY-FOUR

Jackson tugged Alyssa close to his side. Out of town? Not hardly. He needed to call Lockwood.

CoCo appeared at his elbow. "The happy couple is making their way here. Come on." She gently pushed him toward the living room, then headed off toward Luc.

He whispered into Alyssa's ear. "Let's just give our congratulations to Luc's sister and fiancé and then we can go."

She shook her head, but her face still matched the white of her shirt. "He's not going to run me off. Who does he think he is, showing up here?"

"What does Luc's sister look like?" Jackson scanned over people's heads, hoping to single out the engaged couple.

"She's got the bluest eyes you've ever seen, honey-colored hair and an infectious smile. Oh, and she's in a wheelchair."

He glanced about and finally spotted the woman whose smile lit up the entire room. He led Alyssa in that direction.

"Alyssa!" the bright young woman hollered as she spied them. She held out her arms. "It's so good to see you."

Alyssa plastered on a smile and hugged her. "You, too. Felicia Trahan, this is Jackson Devereaux."

He gave a low bow and kissed her hand. "The pleasure is mine." Her blue eyes were hypnotic.

Felicia giggled. "Now, that's a Southern gentleman for you."

"Where's this husband-to-be of yours?" Alyssa asked.

"I don't know. He was just here. Probably went to get me another mint julep. I'm parched." She nodded and smiled as people moved past her. "Did CoCo tell you I'm having my surgery next week?"

"No. What surgery?"

"They're going to operate on my legs. Doctors say I have a seventy-five percent chance of being able to walk." She smiled, happiness shining in her eyes. "I'm determined to have Luc escort me down the aisle."

"Oh, girl, that's great."

"Yeah." Felicia tilted her head. "Oh, there's my man now. Sweetheart, I want you to meet some people."

Alyssa and Jackson turned to greet Felicia's fiancé.

Jackson tipped his head and shook the man's hand. "Hello, Frank."

"Jax."

Alyssa gripped Jackson's arm. "Am I missing something?"

Felicia frowned. "Do you know each other?"

Jackson shifted his weight from one foot to another. "Yeah."

"Jax works on the docks, Licia." Frank moved to stand by her wheelchair. "The sheriff introduced us."

"But I thought you were a reporter, Mr. Devereaux,

yes?" Felicia's brows knitted. "I still don't understand."
Felicia stared up at her fiancé.

Frank whispered something to his bride-to-be, then
narrowed his eyes at Jackson. "So, anything new?"

Jackson gave a curt nod toward the senator. Frank's
eyes widened.

"I need to run to the ladies' room," Alyssa blurted out.

"Oh, down the hall and to the left," Felicia replied.

"I'll walk you," Jackson said. He nodded at the couple.
"We'll see y'all in a few."

They took their leave.

"You could've told me he was helping you," Alyssa
hissed.

"I didn't want to tell anyone." He grasped her elbow.
"You know how dangerous these people are. I couldn't
let his name out for fear they'd go after him."

"You could've told *me*." Hurt wove into her words.

When they turned left at the end of the corridor,
Jackson cast a glance behind them. Frank and Felicia had
already moved to mingle with a group in the middle of
the living room. Jackson took out his BlackBerry and
punched in the number for Agent Lockwood. He waited
as the call rang and went to voice mail. Hanging up, he
dug in his pocket.

"What are you doing?"

"Looking for Agent Olson's number. Lockwood isn't
answering."

"Why?"

"I want to let them know Mouton is here. His wife told
them he was out of town, remember?"

Olson answered on the second ring. After Jackson explained the situation, the ATF officer assured Jackson

that he'd leave that minute. Jackson put away his Black-Berry and held Alyssa's hand. "He's on his way."

"What do we do in the meantime?"

"Act like nothing's wrong. We don't want Mouton to get suspicious and bolt."

Her face twisted into a grimace.

"What?"

"It's still hard to believe he's probably involved in all of this."

"Yeah."

He pulled her into his arms. "*Chère,* we'll get the truth out." Her hair smelled so good. Like wildflowers growing along the country roads of the bayou. He brushed his lips against her temple. His heart surged at the connection.

"I know that, but my emotions are all tied up." She snuggled against his chest.

"Alyssa, there's something we need to talk about."

"Mm-hm." She hadn't opened her eyes yet.

"I think I'm falling in lo—"

"Jackson, there's a man here to see you," Luc said, clearing his throat.

Letting out a frustrated sigh, Jackson released Alyssa. "We're on our way," he told Luc, who nodded and headed down the hall.

"Must be Olson," Alyssa said, her cheeks still bright.

He took her hand and walked beside her. "I'm going to get this out if it kills me."

She laughed, the familiar warmth spreading to his toes. "Seems like we're always getting interrupted."

Just before they entered the living room, he tugged her to a stop and turned her to face him. "This won't wait."

His Adam's apple felt the size of a watermelon. "I think I'm falling in love with you, Alyssa LeBlanc."

He turned and strode into the living room.

Let her simmer about that for a while.

Falling in love with me?

He just blurted it out and walked away. Oh, who did he think he was? Dropping such a bombshell, then leaving?

Yet her heart laughed. He felt the same way about her as she did him. Not only that, he'd been the one to say it.

She followed the path he'd taken, spied him talking with Agent Olson, and moved to stand beside him. She slipped her hand in his and squeezed. He smiled at her, but continued his whispered discussion with the officer.

Uncertainty etched deep into the ATF agent's face. He ran a hand over his crew cut. "I don't want to cause a major scene here." He glanced over the party. "He's sticking to Mrs. Trahan like glue. I need one of you to try and get her away from him. I'd like to avoid involving anyone else, and don't want this to turn ugly."

"Alyssa, can you distract Mrs. Trahan?"

"I can try."

Jackson stood straight. "I'll get Mouton to take a walk with me outside, using my reporter status as enticement."

Agent Olson nodded. "Okay, then." He laid a hand on Alyssa's shoulder. "Ready?"

"I think so. Yeah."

Jackson kissed her so quickly his lips were gone before she registered them on hers. "Be careful." He winked.

Her heart thudded, but not from the excitement of the situation. She straightened her shoulders before walking across the room, weaving around people.

She nodded at the couple as she approached. "Evening, Senator. Hey, Mrs. Trahan, can I talk to you for a sec?" She laid her hand on Hattie's forearm.

"Sure." Hattie studied Alyssa's face. "Are you okay? Is something wrong?"

Alyssa felt, more than saw, Jackson's scrutiny. She forced her voice not to warble. "Everything's fine. I just wanted to ask you something." She racked her mind, searching. "About Luc and CoCo."

"Are they okay?" Hattie's gaze darted around the room.

"They're fine. I just wanted to run something by you right quick." She smiled sweetly at the man responsible for killing her parents. "Will you excuse us a moment?"

Alyssa didn't wait for an answer. She turned Hattie toward the den.

Her part was done. She caught sight of Jackson. He strode toward Senator Mouton, who'd taken a couple of steps to follow them.

"Senator, may I have a quick word with you outside? The *Times-Picayune* is doing an in-depth report on the election." Jackson delivered his lines just loud enough for others to turn and stare at him and Mouton.

Alyssa held her breath and slowly kept leading Hattie. She saw CoCo and Luc talking to a server and headed in their direction. Hattie would most likely be mortified that such a scandal would occur on her property. Her family came from generations of Southern gentry—no disgrace should be mentioned in connection with the Trahan name. Then again, after Justin's arrest a few months ago for murder…

"What are you two up to?" CoCo asked.

"I need to talk to you for a second," Alyssa said.

Hattie jerked her head. "Wait a minute. I thought you said you needed to talk to me about CoCo and Luc?"

"What's going on?" Luc asked.

Oh, no matter how she did this, the end result wouldn't be pretty. Alyssa took a deep sigh and locked stares with her sister. She filled them in on the turn of events. "Agent Olson's here now. Jackson's taking Mouton outside."

"What're y'all talking about? I don't understand. Would somebody please tell me what's happening, yes?" Hattie's hands trembled as she wrung them.

CoCo wrapped an arm around Luc's mother, speaking in hushed tones. Luc glanced toward the French doors leading to the patio. "Maybe I should check and make sure everything's okay."

"I think that'd be a good idea," Alyssa said.

Crack!

A gunshot rang out. Alyssa's blood ran cold.

Jackson!

TWENTY-FIVE

People swarmed in all directions. Women cried out. Men shouted.

Alyssa ran toward the French doors. Luc grabbed her arm, jerking her to a stop.

"I have to see if he's okay." She struggled to break free of Luc's hold. The panic almost choked her. "I need to know. I love him." Sobs ripped from her chest. She shivered.

Luc held her steady. "You won't be much help to him right now. I'll let you know immediately. I promise."

She nodded, shoving the tears from her face.

Luc barged out the French doors. Alyssa couldn't stop herself from going to the doorway.

Images of the sheriff's beaten body flashed across her mind. But it was Jackson's face she saw.

Luc tore across the yard.

Another gunshot split the air.

Without thinking, Alyssa ran onto the patio. Her heart filled her throat.

"Get down," someone yelled.

She turned in the direction of the voice.

"Alyssa!"

Her body quivered at the sound of Jackson's voice.

Rough hands grabbed her from behind. One covered her mouth. "Don't move."

Senator Mouton had her! What?

The cold muzzle of a handgun pressed against her neck.

She froze. She would die, just like her parents. Murdered. By the same man's hand.

"Do exactly what I tell you, and you won't get hurt," the senator growled in her ear. "You're more like your mother than I thought. I'd stuck around only to get the opportunity to take you out quietly, and look at the trouble you've caused for me. I could be on a beach in another country if it weren't for you."

Luc, Jackson and Agent Olson moved toward her, flanking all sides. Jackson's right shirt sleeve had a large red splotch on the shoulder, seeping downward. Had he been shot? Alyssa's stomach dropped to her knees. Her legs turned to oatmeal. She went slack against Mouton.

"Stand up now, or I'll shoot you," he said. "Y'all stay back or I'll kill her." His voice got louder, booming in her ear, a jarring reminder of how quickly a life could end.

The three men halted.

"Let her go, Senator," Jackson said.

Alyssa blinked back fresh tears. She'd die without getting a chance to tell Jackson she loved him. Every nerve in her body tensed into a tight coil.

The French doors burst open. Felicia nudged her wheelchair over the threshold. "Luc?"

Mouton lifted the gun and pointed it directly at Felicia, who gasped and tried to reverse the wheelchair. Frank darted around Felicia, charging the senator.

Senator Mouton fired.

The gunshot reverberated inside Alyssa's head.

"No-o-o-o!"

Frank collapsed to the ground. Jackson and Luc rushed forward, only to be halted by the barrel of Mouton's gun.

"Get out of my way. We're going to walk to my car, nice and slow. None of you make a move, or she's toast."

Oh, God, I know I'm new at this personal relationship with You, but please save me. I don't want to die. There's been too much killing already. Please, God, don't let him shoot me.

Peace as calm as the morning sun touching the bayou filled her. Her legs found muscle. She straightened.

"Come on, move it." The senator shoved her toward the circular driveway, still pressing her body against his, using her as a human shield. "Your mother didn't know when to let things go, either."

She took a shaky step. She glanced to where the three men looked poised to spring. Maybe four feet? She took another step.

"That's right, easy does it." Mouton pushed her toward his car.

If he got her in the vehicle, he'd kill her for sure.

Alyssa took another step, sucked in air and offered up a final silent prayer. Then she rammed her elbow into his gut with every ounce of strength she could muster.

He dropped the gun and fell backward, grunting.

Luc and Agent Olson moved as one. Luc tackled Mouton while Agent Olson grabbed his gun. Jackson seized Alyssa, pulling her to his chest, and twisted them away from the grappling men. "Shh," Jackson whispered against her hair.

"Frank?"

He glanced at the paramedics. "I don't know. But I think it was a heart shot, *chère.*"

"No." She pushed a few inches away from him, tears streaming from her eyes. "I was scared you'd been shot."

He smiled and ran a thumb over her scar. "The senator got Olson's gun away from him and fired off a shot." He glanced at his shoulder. "Just grazed me. Nothing more than a scratch."

"You don't get it. I thought he'd killed you before I…" She couldn't stop the tears from flowing.

"It's okay. We're fine." He enveloped her in a hug.

"I thought I wouldn't get a chance to tell you that I love you."

Agent Olson had hauled Senator Mouton away while a paramedic treated Jackson's shoulder. The local sheriff deputies waited for the coroner to come—the shot to Frank's chest had been fatal. The doctor had given Felicia and Hattie sedatives. Both now slept in their beds. Jackson didn't envy Luc's position. He'd had a hard time consoling his sister. It had taken him and CoCo an hour to get her calmed down before the doctor arrived.

And Hattie? Well, Jackson actually felt sorry for her. She'd been humiliated with the townsfolk over the scenario, but she'd held Felicia while she cried. Maybe they'd work their issues out together.

Agent Lockwood finished taking their statements and put his notebook away. He shoved to his feet. "Once Roger heard we'd busted the senator, he sang like a bird. Implicated Senator Mouton as the designer of the whole plan. Apparently he's been coordinating this arms smuggling for almost two decades—the entire time he's been in office. He was more scared his low-life partners would kill him than he was of our prosecution."

"Which is what our mother discovered." Alyssa stared across the room at CoCo and Tara.

"Yeah. Gocheaux piped in that he and Burl had killed your parents and made it look like an accident. Thibodeaux killed Kevin Arnold. All on Mouton's orders."

"Why would he admit doing such a thing?" Alyssa asked.

Lockwood smiled, but the expression looked forced. "Because he's trying to make himself a sweeter deal. Turning evidence. Burl says he was coerced into cooperating. Threats against his wife."

Jackson snaked his arm around Alyssa's waist. They sat together on the sofa, both perching on the edge of the seat. She snuggled closer.

Standing, Luc extended his hand to the FBI agent. "Guess that wraps it all up."

"We'll need each of you to come by and sign your statements." He nodded to Jackson. "ATF's Internal Affairs will be contacting you for a statement, too."

"For what?" Alyssa asked.

"Because Mouton got Agent Olson's firearm away from him. The senator shot Jackson with a government-registered gun. The agency isn't too keen on situations like that." Agent Lockwood gave a final nod before leaving.

"I'm going to check on Fels." CoCo drew to her feet.

Luc automatically took her arm and moved with her.

Jackson wanted to be alone with Alyssa, to talk about where they went from here, and stood. He held out his hand to her. "Care to walk with me, *chère?*"

She glanced at Tara, who smiled. "I'm gonna start helping the staff pick up. I might want to take some food home. No sense letting good grub go to waste."

Outside, the sun had set. Only the final streaks of

purple stood out against the darkening sky. Jackson took Alyssa into his arms and kissed her, pouring every bit of his heart into the embrace.

He stepped back, cupped her face in his hands and ran his thumb over her scar. "Now, about what you said to me…"

"What?" A smile lifted the corners of her mouth.

"You told me that you loved me."

She arched a single eyebrow. "I did? Are you sure?"

A life with her would be many things, but never boring. Not for one minute. "I'm positive I heard you say that." He tilted his head to the side and tapped his chin with his finger. "Yeah, I'm certain."

"Well, if you're sure, then."

"But it wouldn't hurt anything to hear you say it again. Just so I don't forget."

"I love you, Jackson Devereaux." She smiled softly, those eyes of hers dancing.

He pulled her closer and rested his forehead against hers. "And I love you, *chère*."

* * * * *

Trouble's brewing in Lagniappe, Louisiana:
BAYOU JUDGMENT
Robin Caroll's next
Steeple Hill Love Inspired Suspense
On sale in May, 2008 from Steeple Hill Books.

Dear Reader,

Welcome back to Cajun country! South Louisiana has such a wonderful and diverse culture, different from other Southern states. With bayous, intercoastal ports and rice plants, it's the perfect setting for this bayou series.

I've loved continuing the story of the LeBlanc family, with their rich Cajun culture and Southern heritage. Penning each book is a bit like going home for me, and I thank you for journeying with me.

Like Alyssa, I struggled for quite some time with building a personal relationship with Jesus. Some of her lessons learned are mine. I hope her story will encourage and uplift you.

I love hearing from readers. Please visit me at www.robincaroll.com and drop me a line, or write to me at PO Box 242091, Little Rock, AR, 72223. Join my newsletter group…sign my guest book. I look forward to hearing from you.

Blessings,

Robin Caroll

QUESTIONS FOR DISCUSSION

1. Alyssa detested the bayou—fought to remove every reminder of her roots from her life. Have you ever felt that way about where you're from? How did you deal with your feelings?

2. Jackson could have turned his quest to bring his friend's attackers to justice into vigilantism. Have you ever experienced feelings of avenging a friend being wronged? How did you handle the situation? Why didn't Jackson take the wrong path?

3. Though her sister didn't worship the way she did, Alyssa noticed a peace and calmness about her sister that brought up questions of her own spiritual path. How can we be the "salt of the earth" to others?

4. Alyssa had to learn to let go of the past in order to move forward in her life. Are there some issues you're dealing with from the past that you need to let go? What Scripture can you find to help you in this area?

5. Jackson and Alyssa had to muddle through several conflicts before they could embrace their love for one another. Have you ever had a relationship run amok because of emotional conflicts? What did you do?

6. Learning that her parents had been murdered devastated Alyssa. How have you dealt with the loss of a loved one in your life?

7. Alyssa felt personal betrayal because of Senator Mouton's involvement in her parents' murder. Have you ever felt betrayed by someone you trusted? How did you move past the pain?

8. Even among her family Alyssa felt like a misfit. Have you ever felt like an outsider? How did you cope with your feelings?

9. Despite her wanting to honor her mother's memory, Alyssa realized she didn't want to be a reporter. Have you ever pursued something, only to realize it wasn't a path you needed to follow? What did you do?

10. Alyssa's dreams were actually blocked memories resurfacing. Have you ever had dreams that revealed a certain truth you'd tried to ignore? How did you deal with the revelation?

INTRODUCING

Love Inspired.

HISTORICAL

A NEW TWO-BOOK SERIES.

Every month, acclaimed
inspirational authors
will bring you engaging stories
rich with romance, adventure
and faith set in a variety
of vivid historical times.

History begins on **February 12**
wherever you buy books.

Steeple
Hill®

LIHLAUNCH

www.SteepleHill.com

REQUEST YOUR FREE BOOKS!

2 FREE RIVETING INSPIRATIONAL NOVELS
PLUS 2 FREE MYSTERY GIFTS

Love Inspired®
SUSPENSE

YES! Please send me 2 FREE Love Inspired® Suspense novels and my 2 FREE mystery gifts. After receiving them, if I don't wish to receive any more books, I can return the shipping statement marked "cancel." If I don't cancel, I will receive 4 brand-new novels every month and be billed just $3.99 per book in the U.S. or $4.74 per book in Canada, plus 25¢ shipping and handling per book and applicable taxes, if any*. That's a savings of 20% off the cover price! I understand that accepting the 2 free books and gifts places me under no obligation to buy anything. I can always return a shipment and cancel at any time. Even if I never buy another book from Steeple Hill, the two free books and gifts are mine to keep forever.

123 IDN EL5H 323 IDN ELQH

Name	(PLEASE PRINT)	
Address		Apt. #
City	State/Prov.	Zip/Postal Code

Signature (if under 18, a parent or guardian must sign)

Order online at www.LoveInspiredSuspense.com

Or mail to Steeple Hill Reader Service™:

IN U.S.A.: P.O. Box 1867, Buffalo, NY 14240-1867
IN CANADA: P.O. Box 609, Fort Erie, Ontario L2A 5X3

Not valid to current Love Inspired Suspense subscribers.

**Want to try two free books from another series?
Call 1-800-873-8635 or visit www.morefreebooks.com**

* Terms and prices subject to change without notice. NY residents add applicable sales tax. Canadian residents will be charged applicable provincial taxes and GST. This offer is limited to one order per household. All orders subject to approval. Credit or debit balances in a customer's account(s) may be offset by any other outstanding balance owed by or to the customer. Please allow 4 to 6 weeks for delivery.

> **Your Privacy:** Steeple Hill is committed to protecting your privacy. Our Privacy Policy is available online at www.eHarlequin.com or upon request from the Reader Service. From time to time we make our lists of customers available to reputable firms who may have a product or service of interest to you. If you would prefer we not share your name and address, please check here. ☐

LISUS07